ROYAL

FEYLAND BOOK 5

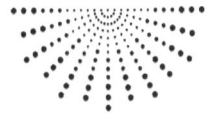

ANTHEA SHARP

Fiddlehead Press

COPYRIGHT

PROLOGUE

THE NEWLY MADE GIRL STOOD, dazed, before the terrible majesty of the Dark Queen of the Realm of Faerie. About her, the creatures of the court laughed and whispered, and the girl wrapped her arms about herself, unsure of this odd new body she inhabited. Her thin dress of silvery gauze lay lightly on her skin, providing little protection from the foreign touch of the air. She sucked a painful breath into her lungs, and tried not to tremble at the strangeness of the world.

"You." The queen leaned forward from the tangled briars of her throne, and pointed one long, pale finger at the girl. Her eyes were deep midnight, and diamonds sparkled like stars in her black hair. "I should strike you down where you stand, for aiding my enemies."

If the girl had done such a thing, she recalled nothing of it. Only confused images of a bright red berry and a net, the terrible transformation, and running through dark woods, something horrifying in pursuit.

"Forgive me, your majesty," she whispered.

A bright-eyed, tangle-haired sprite tumbled into the clearing before the Dark Queen's throne. Standing, he gave her a flourishing bow, one foot pointed on the velvet green mosses.

"Your majesty," he said. "Might I speak?"

The queen let out a sigh, the sound like a wind stirring the empty branches of winter oaks.

"Puck," she said. "You have the freedom of the courts, much as it may displease my mood. Say your piece."

"Yon maid, all unwitting, played but a part in a quest. She does not deserve death—and there are few enough fey folk that her loss, though a small thing, would be felt within the realm."

"Banishment, then, shall be her fate," the queen declared. "To the Shadowlands."

The denizens of the court shivered, the girl most of all. Even she, hiding within her watery dwelling, had heard of that dire place where souls wandered, lost and alone, into eternity.

Though the words might stumble on her tongue, she must plead her case.

"My queen." She bowed as best she might on the unsteady stalks of her legs. "I beg you, do not banish me. Surely there is some way to mend the harm I might have done?"

The denizens of the court whispered, and the girl was glad she could not hear what they said. She had no doubt they suggested dire and dreadful remedies.

"Perchance there might be." The queen narrowed her eyes, then gestured. "Bard Thomas, attend."

A man stepped from the shadows. Silver strands ran through his brown hair, and his eyes were wise and weary beyond measure. "Yes, my queen?"

"How best might I use this youngling in service to the court?"

The bard regarded the girl for a long moment. Sparks and promises flashed in his eyes, and she did not know whether to be hopeful or afraid.

"Send her into the human world, where she might sway mortals to stray into the realm," he said at last. "She can repay her debt by helping ensure that humans will cross over to the Dark Court when they enter the game of Feyland."

The queen gave a single shake of her head. "I mislike having to sacrifice yet another of my handmaidens simply to send a near-useless creature into the mortal realm. Your counsel pleases me not, bard."

"Milady." Puck sprang into the air and hovered there. "The girl has already been touched, though lightly, by the human world. I may be able to slip her through the gateway without further bloodshed. And if not"—he gave an elaborate shrug—"then do with her as you please."

"Your magic is fickle," the queen said.

"Yet you know it cannot be turned to your ends." Puck laughed and flipped in the air, landing once again on the soft ground. "I will attempt to send the maid through."

The queen leaned back, the pale moonlight illuminating her beauty. Overhead, stars sprinkled the edges of the sky, and a night wind stirred the oak leaves into whispering. The girl's nerves hummed as she awaited her fate. Her heartbeat pounded within her chest until she was nearly dizzy from the rhythm.

"Very well," the queen said. She beckoned to the girl, who came forward on shaking limbs. "I lay a *geas* upon you, youngling. From now until the summer wanes, you are charged with leading as many humans as you might toward the magic of the Dark Court so that the realm may be replenished. Should you return without success, the Shadowlands will be your new home."

The girl bowed her head. There was no arguing, and no agreement. When the queen spoke, her word was law.

Behind the tangled throne, gossamer-winged faerie maidens cast pitying glances at the girl. A nearby band of goblins cackled, clearly pleased by the girl's plight. The queen held up one hand and called forth her magic. In a burst of violet light, a silver medallion appeared. It swung, dangling on a chain of silver from the queen's fingers.

"Take this," she said, thrusting the medallion at the girl. "It is your passage back to the realm—but do not call upon it until Lughnasa is nigh."

The girl took the medallion. It was cool against her fingers, the silver disc inset with a pale moonstone, the edges inscribed with runes. She folded it into her palm, proof of the journey she must now undertake.

"Away with her," the queen said to Puck.

Without a further glance at the girl, she signaled for elderberry wine and music. The creatures of her court bestirred themselves, returning to their dancing and feasting.

"Come, maid," Puck said.

The girl did not look behind her as they left the clearing of the Dark Court, though the strains of a plaintive jig followed her into the shimmering darkness beneath the trees.

"I am afraid," she said, once the sounds of the court had faded.

"You are wise to be so," Puck said. "Yet who knows what doors might open to you in the human world?"

CHAPTER ONE

IT HAD TAKEN her a fortnight and three days more to find her way about the human world. Now the girl sat cross-legged, enclosed by the ruined walls of the shelter she'd claimed. The chill of the stained concrete floor did not bother her. One section of the roof jutted overhead, intact enough to keep out the worst of the wind while still revealing a wide swath of sky. Morning clouds and their early chill had shredded away. Weak sunshine straggled in through the gaping holes in the plaster walls. The light was strange, filtered to an oily yellow by the layer of smog hanging over the city.

The few trees remaining in the derelict neighborhood had rotted from within. Some, like the withered sentinel standing outside her wall, still bore lifeless brown leaves that rattled in the breeze. Thin grass grew in the cracks of the cement, the only sign that spring lay across the land.

The regular residents of Crestview had abandoned this part of the city. Now it was inhabited by roaming packs of mortal boys who reminded her of hungry, feral creatures.

Husk-empty women shuffled through the crumbling streets. A building two blocks away housed a clan of yellow-eyed smoke drifters, who dove deep into maniacal dreams even when awake.

The air smelled of decay and hopelessness, of mildew and rot. They called it the Exe, and it was the perfect place to hide.

Under the partial overhang of the roof, she'd made a sleeping pallet mounded with soft blankets. A small wooden chest, bound round with enchantments, contained the precious medallion she had brought from the realm. Strewn about her was a collection of devices essential to navigating her new world. Tablets and messagers and a vid display, effortlessly liberated from the cluttered stores where such things were sold. Scavenged packing boxes held clothing and cosmetics and the sundry items a human girl needed.

But she was not human, and this was not a true home.

Shivers chased over her at the thought that she might never return to the realm—that she would fail and be banished forever to the Shadowlands. She took two fistfuls of her long black hair, and tugged anxiously. Yet, despite her small powers, she must accomplish her required task.

The first step was to become as human as possible. She had chosen a name, a mortal one in two parts, as was their custom. Brea Cairgead. She rolled the syllables about her tongue.

"My name is Brea," she said aloud. "Brea Cairgead. Pleased to meet you. Yes, I am from Eire. Ireland, as you call it. Would you like something to drink?"

She would not be entertaining guests, but the words were a standard part of the vids she'd memorized in her effort to camouflage herself. Early on, she'd realized she must claim to come from a foreign land. She smiled briefly. No one would guess how very far away she was from her homeland.

It was the day of the moon. Monday. A fitting day to begin, and indeed, she could delay no longer. Too long had passed since her arrival, and the ice of the queen's impatience chilled the air, discernible even in the mortal world. Brea snatched up her newest tablet, then conjured a plastic card with her human name and semblance—identification, they called it—and tucked it in the pocket of her sweater.

She must be careful to seem human from this moment on. No more using her magic to transport herself from place to place. The clothing she wore must be made of worldly substance, not woven of starlight and shadows. Although she could drink liquids in this place—indeed, if she did not, she would shrivel from thirst—she could not eat of the food. But she would pretend to do so.

Today, she was a mortal girl.

Roy Lassiter tapped his fingers on the shiny edge of his tablet and let the droning voice of his history teacher, Ms. Lewis, wash over him. He lounged back in his chair, but couldn't get comfortable no matter how far he stretched his legs. Usually he paid more attention in class—World History was one of the two subjects he actually enjoyed, the other being Art—but today, everything felt wrong.

Although it was May, the air held a chilly snap reminiscent of late winter. The scent of decay crept along the halls of

Crestview High, mingling with the fake lemon smell of industrial disinfectant. The students' voices carried strangely, as if underwater.

Roy skimmed his gaze over his classmates. Everyone looked the same as ever: alternately bored, attentive, doodling with one finger, taking diligent notes, or staring out the windows. Nobody else seemed to feel as though the normalcy of the day had turned on its edge, a sharp blade of strangeness cutting through the world.

Once, he would have shrugged it off, ignored the prickle at the back of his neck. But he'd seen freaky things in the last year. Battling nightmare monsters and traveling deep into a fantastical realm tended to give a person a different perspective, and he'd started to trust his instincts.

And his friends.

The shrill signal of the lunch bell at the end of class made him jump. He tucked his tablet away, then joined the throng in the hall, following the hot, damp smell of overcooked gravy. The cafeteria rang with voices as he veered toward the back table where his friends sat.

Such a mixed bunch. Tam Linn, former Exie and still poorer than dirt. Marny Fanalua, strong-willed, big-boned, marginally better off than Tam. And pale, blonde Jennet Carter, the only one he might have predicted hanging with. Like him, she had an embedded wrist-chip that gave her easy credit access, instant recognition as part of the better class, and admission in and out of The View—the specially designed development where they both lived.

Unfortunately, the school at The View hadn't yet been

completed when he and his mom had relocated. At first, he'd despised going to Crestview High. He had the best tech gadgets and drove a grav-car, his house talked to him, and his every need was taken care of. His mom was the freakin' CEO of VirtuMax, the corporation that had moved its operations to Crestview and now dominated the town. No way did he belong among townies who couldn't even afford their own tablets.

Eventually, he'd decided some of the regular town kids were all right, but those from the Exe, the slum, he wouldn't bother talking to.

It had taken him a while to shed that attitude. Marny would probably argue it wasn't gone yet, and she might be right. But only a little.

"Hey," he said, sliding onto the bench beside Marny and tossing his chef-packed lunch on the table.

Tam nodded hello across the graffiti-etched surface, and Jennet smiled a greeting.

"Does the day seem weird to you?" she asked.

"Yeah. Severely."

The anxiety inside him notched down. Whatever was going on, the four of them could deal with it. Even though his old friends couldn't understand, and no way could he explain, he was bound to these three by something bigger than status or popularity.

"Do you think it has to do with the Realm of Faerie?" Marny asked. "That kind of weird?"

"Maybe," Tam said.

"You're the Feyguard," Marny said. "Aren't you supposed to know?"

"It's hard to explain." Jennet shivered, and Tam slid his arm around her shoulders.

The two of them were a solid couple, for sure. It was a classic story—underdog boy gets the rich girl. For a while, Roy'd had his eye on Jennet, and couldn't believe she would choose spoilage from the Exe over someone from her own world.

Finally, he'd come to terms with it, and even gotten to like Tam, but that didn't stop him from wanting a girlfriend. Loneliness was a quiet ache underpinning his life. Mostly, he ignored it, but sometimes it was hard, especially when Tam and Jennet went all lovey in front of him.

"It was freakishly cold this morning," Marny said. "Maybe a big storm is blowing in."

"No." Roy opened his lunch and pulled out a turkey pesto gourmet sandwich. "Whatever this is, it's not a natural part of this world." He leaned over the table and lowered his voice. "I think it's magic."

"Think it's a faerie attack?" Jennet asked, setting down her water bottle to give him a worried look.

"Not a direct one," Tam said. "We closed the gateway enough that the fey folk can't get through."

"Things might have changed," Roy said. "Let's meet in-game after school to check it out. Maybe someone stumbled into the realm by accident."

Through some strange mixing of the worlds, the gate connecting the mortal world to the realm was accessed through the immersive virtual game of Feyland. Feyland—which happened to be VirtuMax's top project. The fact that the game contained a secret portal to a place where magic really existed was a helluva secret to keep from his mom.

Luckily, Dr. Lassiter was always preoccupied with her work. As long as Roy stayed out of trouble, she didn't pay much attention to his life. He had one more year at home, and then... well, then was then. Right now, he had bigger issues to deal with.

"All this would be a lot simpler if the Elder Fey just shut the gate," Marny said, balling up her paper napkin.

"The Realm of Faerie would wither away without at least a trickle of mortal energy," Tam said.

"Soul-suckers, if you ask me." Marny shot her napkin into the trash can. She never missed.

"Humans need that touch of magic," Roy said, surprising himself. "This world's bleak enough—imagine if nothing magical could get through."

Okay, maybe his opinion wasn't that surprising. One of these days, he was going to share his art files and show the rest of the Feyguard the drawings he'd been making. Pictures inspired by what they'd seen: ethereal maidens with gossamer wings, fearsome goblins wearing blood-red caps, a mist-lit glade under an enchanted midnight moon.

Art is for girls. Stop doodling and do something useful. Most artists go on to kill themselves, anyway. The mocking voices in his head were quiet whispers—but never silent.

"I'll message Spark," Jennet said. "Maybe she'll have an idea about what's going on."

Spark Jaxley, the professional gamer, was another Feyguard—one of the handful of humans charged with guarding the boundary between the worlds. Roy had crushed on her hard, but she'd paired up with a guy named Aran.

Win some, lose some. Too bad Roy mostly seemed to be losing.

At least he had his friends, and the challenge of the Feyguard to keep him busy. Though being a hero wasn't nearly as fun if you couldn't tell anybody about it. Not that the other students would believe him.

Roy glanced around the cafeteria, at all the preoccupied faces, everyone busy with their own fears and hopes and lives. Once, he'd had the entire school eating out of his hand. He couldn't walk into a room without girls flocking to him. The teachers had adored him, the guys wanted to be best buds. He'd been the glorious sun at the center of the Crestview High solar system.

It had been hollow, but the surface rush was great—until he'd had to pay the price. Sometimes the memories twisted hard inside his chest when he recalled how it felt to straddle the world. Triumphant, unable to lose.

Special.

"Anybody home?" Marny jabbed his shoulder.

"What?"

"Stop staring into space, and pay attention."

"I am." He rubbed his shoulder. Marny had a fierce poke.

"Tam and I'll meet you after school," Jennet said. "Your house is the best place to sim together—especially if something's tweaked."

Nobody else owned multiple FullD machines, let alone ones linked up in the same room. Being surrounded with prime gear was one of the perks of being the VirtuMax CEO's son. Too bad most of the advantages were tech-related. His mom was still the work-obsessed, cold woman she'd been his whole life. His dad—whom he hadn't seen in seven months— kept saying he'd come join them in Crestview, but Roy wasn't holding his breath.

"Sounds good," he said, and managed a smile. "Meet up after school. Right."

It was something real to do, other than half-ass his homework and hide his artwork from his mom. He wasn't sure they'd find any answers, but at least it would give his afternoon a sense of meaning.

CHAPTER TWO

Brea swallowed back her frustration, though impatience hummed through her. The air of the mortal high school pressed, thick and too warm, against her skin. She leaned over the scratched counter of the front office, bringing every bit of her small persuasive magic to bear. She had not been prepared for the complexities of what the humans called "bureaucracy."

"I am certain I am enrolled into the school," she lied. "With all the necessary forms completed." She pushed the words at the man behind the counter, giving them the force of belief.

"Spell your name again," the secretary said, shoving his glasses up his nose and staring at the display in front of him.

Brea did, finally managing to brush her fingers against the back of the screen. *I am a student here*, she thought fiercely.

"Ah, there we are." The secretary tapped his keyboard. "Do you have your own tablet, or do you need a school-provided one?"

"I have this." She set her new tablet on the counter.

The secretary raised one eyebrow. "Keep it close. High-end items like that tend to disappear here."

"Disappear?"

"You think we run people through security to get in here just for fun? Listen, Miss Care... Miss Keerg—"

"Cairgead."

He waved his hand. "I don't know what you're used to, but Crestview has a lot of rough places. And rough kids to go with it. Watch your step around here—and make sure to stay out of the Exe. Absolutely worst part of town."

"Thank you."

She forced herself not to laugh. There was nothing in her habitation that frightened her, or was beyond her powers to deal with.

He tapped at his screen a moment more, then sat back.

"You're all taken care of," he said. "Schedule should ping over to your tablet. The day's almost over, but you can still make your last class. PreCalc, Room 115—down the hall. I'll let Mr. Brinksea know you're on the way."

Brea nodded her thanks, then took her tablet. With the watchful gaze of the secretary at her back, she headed into the depths of Crestview High. Her shoes squeaked over the waxed vinyl floor, and the harsh scent of artificial fruit stung her nose.

She read the numbers on the plain wooden doors and caught glimpses of the students within as she passed. Panic slowly built in her throat, until her breath came in short gasps. She might fear no mortals who stumbled across her in the Exe, but now she was entering the heart of enemy territory, and it seemed sheer foolishness.

If only she had remained slumbering in the watery shadows, instead of being lured out by a bright berry. If only the queen had not charged her with this impossible task and thrust her from the realm.

Certainly her quarry was here—those mortals most likely to be swayed into the Dark Realm of Feyland. So here she must be, through danger of discovery, and death. Humans feared the strangeness she represented.

No. She forced herself to take a breath, though the air shook within her lungs.

Had she not studied intently for this role? She glanced down at her boots, her jeans, her shirt and sweater chosen in the newest style. Her dark hair was bound back with shiny clips, and her face held a touch of cosmetics. She was young. Newly born in some ways, filled with the ripples of decades in others. Yet she looked the part of a mortal teenager well. No one would suspect what she was.

And the halls of the school were where she must do her work. Pushing back her fear, Brea opened the door numbered 115.

"...solving for that function." The teacher turned to look at her. His blue eyes were keen behind his glasses, and his hair was leached of color at the temples, denoting his age. "You're the new student, I presume?"

"Yes. Brea Cairgead."

"Come in, grab a seat. There's one at the back table, beside Royal Lassiter. Move over, Lassiter."

A brown-haired young man scooted his chair over, then patted the empty one beside him.

"Here," he said, smiling.

She blinked, unprepared for the effect of his human smile. It caused a strange sensation within her, as if she had swallowed a bee and it was buzzing inside her chest. Ducking her head, she hurried to the indicated chair and sat.

"Don't worry," he said quietly. "I don't bite. At least, not on the first day."

She could hear the smile lingering in his voice, and carefully peeked up to see him regarding her. His eyes were brown. Not mud brown, but rather the gold-flecked current of a forest stream.

"I'm Roy," he said. "You don't talk much, do you?"

"I am Brea," she said.

By the moon and stars, she was not nearly as prepared for the mortal world as she had thought. Not when a mortal boy could stumble her tongue and knot her fingers with a single look.

"Lassiter," the teacher called, "stop flirting with the new girl. Help her find the right screen, and let's all get back to work."

"Here." Roy leaned over and tapped her tablet, then scrolled through. "We're on this page."

He smelled like spice and salt, and distraction.

"I see," she said.

Brea did not offer thanks. It was not the custom of the fey. Indeed, to thank a creature was to offend them greatly. She tilted the glowing tablet screen and tried not to feel his gaze lingering on her.

Far better to be unseen, unremarkable. Quickly, she drew a spell of deflection about herself. She was flickering shadow. She was wind ruffling the water.

To her surprise, Roy did not look away, as every other human had when she used magic to turn aside unwanted attention. Instead, his regard sharpened.

"Where are you from?" he asked, with more than idle curiosity.

"Ireland." The lie trembled against her tongue.

"Exchange student? Who's your host family?"

"Pay attention back there." The teacher's voice was brusque. "Do I need to reassign your seat?"

"Fine." Roy held up a placating hand and leaned back into his chair.

Brea took a slow breath, trying to calm the flutter of her nerves. There was something dangerous about Roy Lassiter. She sensed it, the way prey felt the heavy vibrations of a hunter's tread even before the danger was visible. Already, she had erred by drawing his notice.

"To continue," the teacher said, "in this function of x, we are solving for the second degree polynomial equation."

She stared at the incomprehensible figures scribed upon her tablet. Beside her, she could feel Roy Lassiter's attention upon her. Her heart beat fast under that scrutiny, though she did not make the mistake of looking at him again.

The screen glowed up at her, and she traced the numeric patterns with one finger.

She had long since learned to heed her instincts—and they spoke now of peril. Though her magic did not mesh well with mortal technology, she would spend the effort to change her class schedule.

It was best if she did not pursue this particular branch of

mathematics—especially not seated next to this boy who jangled her senses so completely.

After school, Roy leaned against the dingy bricks of Crestview High's main building, letting the faint warmth of spring soak into his shoulders. The frost of the morning had faded, banished by the strengthening sun.

Six more weeks until the school year ended. Then one more long year in Crestview before he could leave this town and get his real life started.

So what if he didn't have a clue what that might be? At least he knew it didn't have anything to do with computers or business. His mom kept pushing him that direction, and she could pull some serious strings.

As recently as a few months ago, he'd been fine with the idea of letting the Lassiter name and VirtuMax connection open doors to top business and programming schools. But now it felt wrong. Not only because he didn't want to coast in on his mom's connections, but wrong as in not a good fit for him.

He'd already lived a lie once, and it had ended with him almost trapped in the Realm of Faerie forever. If not for Tam and Jennet, he'd still be in the Bright Court, servant to the king.

So, he knew he didn't want to be a clone of his mom, groomed to take over the corporation. And nice as it was to have more than enough money, he was starting to suspect that getting everything he ever wanted hadn't done him any favors.

It sure hadn't gotten him interesting girls.

Maybe because you aren't interesting. The annoying voice in his head sounded like Marny. Roy shoved it down, then turned to greet Jennet and Tam.

"Ready?" Jennet asked, slinging her satchel over her shoulder.

"Hold on," Roy said, still scanning the students coming out of the building.

"Who are you looking for?" Tam asked.

"New girl named Brea. Long, dark hair, pale skin. Is she in class with either of you guys?"

Jennet shook her head, but Tam looked thoughtful.

"Maybe," he said. "There's supposed to be a new student in my Spanish class, but she wasn't there today. Why?"

"Not sure." Even now, the memory of what, exactly, had intrigued him about her was fading. No more students exited the building, and Roy shrugged. "Anyway—you guys ready?"

Without waiting for a reply, he led them to the parking lot, where his shiny red grav-car waited. He'd gotten in the habit of offering Jennet a ride up to The View, and Tam too, on his internship days. Luckily, they were all free to play this afternoon.

For fun, he peeled out of the parking lot. Driving too fast bugged Jennet, which therefore bugged Tam. But Roy's heart wasn't in it—he was just keeping up appearances.

His whole life was that way, really, but he didn't know how to stop. Or who he'd be, if he did.

"What do you think we'll find in-game?" he asked.

"Things have been pretty quiet," Jennet said. "Since we closed the gateway."

"Again." Tam's voice was dry.

"Not that that's a bad thing," Jennet added. "I'd be just as glad if we don't ever have to battle the Dark Queen again."

Tam reached forward from the back seat and squeezed her shoulder. Sometimes they were so sweet to each other, it made Roy queasy. He focused on the road up to Crestview, the houses on either side becoming larger, the landscaping better, until they flashed under the plas-metal arch that marked the entrance to The View.

The already big houses turned grandiose, true mansions complete with fountains and landscaping. The biggest place, of course, belonged to the Lassiters. It was set at the edge of the bluff overlooking Crestview, and boasted a swimming pool and tennis court (mostly unused), a five-car garage, and several thousand square feet of inlaid stone floors and meticulously decorated rooms. The fancy wrought-iron gate barring the driveway rolled back at their approach, and Roy slipped the grav-car into his space in the garage.

The three of them piled out and HANA, the House-Activated Network Assistant, remotely opened the door leading into the house.

"*Welcome home, Royal,*" the metallic computer voice said. "*I see you have brought your usual guests. Kitchen staff has been alerted.*"

Jennet wrinkled her nose at him. "Aren't you ever going to change the voice on your network?"

"It's my mom's pick," he said. "It's not so bad."

He'd never really thought about it, but he supposed the

standard voice was fairly cold and inflectionless. Jennet and her dad had their HANA set to some woman's voice. But it was just a network, so why pretend it was anything more?

"House, have them send food down to the theater," he said.

The staff was good about providing snacks for him and his friends. He supposed it gave them something to do to liven up their days.

"Playing our main avatars?" he asked as he led Tam and Jennet down the dimly lit hall to the theater.

"That would be best," Tam said. "Since we don't know what we're going to find in-game."

"If everything checks out, we can hop on our alternates," Jennet said. "I'm having fun learning how to play my Knight."

She grinned at Tam. His main character was a Knight, and he was a damn good fighter. So was Roy, of course, though his Mercenary character had a few different skills. They'd fought plenty of duels in-game, and were evenly matched. At least on those characters.

For their alts, Tam had chosen an Archer. Roy, to everyone's surprise, including his own, had made an Illuminer—a new character type introduced after the Beta testing.

"Really?" Jennet had said, then blushed. "I mean—that's a different choice for you. A hybrid caster..."

"Who draws with light." Tam gave him a considering look. "Interesting choice."

"I have hidden depths," Roy had said.

Maybe someday he'd figure out what those depths actually were. But his friends hadn't given him any more hardship about his choice, and he was enjoying finding out what his new character could do.

The tall double doors at the end of the hall whooshed open as they got close. Roy barely glanced at the banks of equipment and gaming systems as they stepped into the theater. His mom was a collector, and had almost every machine and system ever invented, from the early low-rez games up through motion captures and surround setups.

The top-end simulators were kept in a special area. He keyed open the glass panels separating the FullD systems from the rest of the room. There used to be three systems, but he talked his mom into adding a fourth, so that if and when Spark came to visit, they could all sim together. He paused, one hand on the cool glass, and frowned. They'd need five now that Aran was in the picture, and not looking like he was leaving anytime soon. Not since he got a job with VirtuMax. And hooked up with Spark.

Roy gave himself a mental shake. He'd had his chance with her, and had messed it up somehow, before they'd even got to a first date. Probably his fault, judging by the hollow feeling in his gut—a feeling he shoved away. Damn, he really was veering toward the emo side.

Good thing they were back on their mains today. He could immerse himself in the straightforward hack-n-slash character of his Mercenary.

Jennet took the newer system in the middle, and Tam and Roy flanked her, leaving the brand-new FullD unmanned.

Roy glanced at it. "Do you think Marny—"

"Nope," Tam said.

"But she—"

"Only because you tricked her." Jennet raised her finger at him. "You know she's highly claustrophobic about simming.

Don't think we haven't tried talking her around. We all know she'd be a great addition to the Feyguard."

"Not if she won't sim," Tam said. "Her choice—respect it."

"As the game goes worldwide, we're going to need more help," Roy said. "Don't you think? I mean, six of us guarding the border between the mortal and faerie realms?"

"If the Elder Fey decide we need more, they'll do something," Tam said.

"Right. We're talking about sleeping magical beings two realities removed from our world. Not sure they'll stay on top of all developments."

"Less argue, more play," Jennet said. "Gear up, guys. We can discuss this later."

She was right. Fun as it was to snipe with Tam, they had a job to do. Without further talk, they donned gaming helmets, slid on sensor-equipped gloves, and slipped into their contoured sim chairs.

"See you in there," Roy said, activating the icon for Feyland.

Gateway, he thought, holding the image in his mind so the system would pick it up. Weird as that seemed.

It had taken them some time to figure out how to move around the various levels of Feyland as it connected with the Realm of Faerie. A lot of it was pure will—telling the game where they needed to go, and then hoping like hell it would take them there. It was one form of magic, he supposed.

The game rushed up at him through the sim interface. No matter how often he was prepared for the sickening swirl of golden light that marked the transition into the realm, it still made his stomach churn. He pulled in a deep breath through his nose, and then his character materialized in-game.

His Mercenary wore gleaming bronze armor, and had a gigantic sword strapped to his back. Beside him, Tam and Jennet's characters appeared. Tam's silver armor glowed, and Jennet wore the blue robes of her Spellcaster, one hand gripping a tall wooden staff with a crystal set in the end.

They stood in a clearing surrounded by tall trees with pale trunks. Late afternoon light slanted through the greenish-silver leaves, and a soft breeze wove through the air, stirring a lock of Jennet's hair. The usual ring of mushrooms encircled them, a blend of spindle-stalked, pale fungus and bright red mushrooms with white-speckled caps.

This was the game world, but on either side of their clearing stood two mirror-image faerie glades that only the Feyguard could see.

To their left, the clearing blazed with light, making the white-spotted mushrooms of the faerie ring glow. A golden bird swooped through the air, singing, and the fey shimmer of pixies danced in the green-leafed trees. That way led to the Bright Court. Despite its pleasant aspect, there was plenty of danger along that road.

The glade to their right was touched with twilight, the faerie ring made entirely of the moon-pale mushrooms and surrounded by dark evergreens. A crow called through the dusky air, and the first few stars of night glittered above the treetops. That way lay a place Roy would happily never visit again: The Dark Court.

Unfortunately, if something had crossed into the mortal world, it would come from there.

Jennet nimbly jumped over the ring of mushrooms and went to the side of the clearing connected to the Dark Court. Tam was right behind her, and Roy followed.

"You guys see anything?" she asked.

Roy lifted one gauntleted hand and ran it along the invisible wall between the worlds. He took a couple of steps, then paused when his fingers encountered an irregularity.

"The crack is here," he said. "Doesn't seem any wider."

Tam straightened from where he'd been inspecting the mossy ground. "I don't see any signs of passage. The salt we sprinkled across the boundary seems undisturbed."

Roy still wasn't convinced that a line of salt would prove an effective barrier to a determined fey creature, but Jennet swore by the lore in her old book, *Tales of Folk and Faerie*. So they'd poured salt all the way around the clearing. At the very least, if something crossed over it might scatter the line and give them some warning.

Jennet lifted her mage staff and a bluish glow spread from the crystal. Under that light, the wall became visible as glowing lines of computer code enclosing the middle clearing.

"I'm not Aran, but he showed me what to look for," she said. "I don't see any breaks in the code."

Tam set his hand on the pommel of his sword and frowned at the wall. "So either it's intact, and we're jumping at shadows, or something got out somehow."

"If a creature escaped the realm, it would have to be a small one," Roy said. "Something that could slip through a teensy crack without changing anything."

"Or something so strong it can erase the signs of its passage," Tam said.

"So it's either very weak—or very powerful. Great." Jennet tugged on the stray wisp of her hair.

"At least we don't have to close the gateway again," Roy said.

"Yet." Tam stared at the glowing code.

Roy ran his hands over the wall again. The thin seam was barely a bump beneath his questing fingers.

"Seems okay," he said.

"We should enter the Dark Realm anyway," Tam said. "Just to make sure."

Jennet's throat moved as she swallowed, but she didn't say anything.

"Yeah," Roy said. He didn't like it, but Tam was right. "If anything came through, it probably came from there, and not the Bright Court."

Unlike the Dark Queen, the Bright King seemed content to let little wisps of magic through, and take only the small bits of mortal dreamings that made their way to him.

At least, *now* he did. When the game was first in prototype, the king had snared Roy and used him as his agent in the mortal world.

Roy shook his head. He'd been an idiot back then, invulnerable in his arrogance. It had nearly cost the three of them their lives.

Together, they moved to face the dim clearing. Jennet stepped between him and Tam and grabbed their hands.

"On three," she said. "One. Two. Three."

They pressed forward, and aching cold seared Roy. It wasn't easy to pass through the wall, but as Feyguard, they could do so. Though he didn't much enjoy the harsh discomfort, it was part of the job.

The pale mushrooms flared as they stepped over the boundary of the faerie ring leading to the Dark Court. Above them, the pine boughs stirred restlessly. A sliver of moon shone, bright and sharp, in the darkening sky.

Clenching his jaw, Roy held back the shiver that wanted to shake through him. Ominous shadows stirred deeper in the forest. The Dark Realm awaited.

CHAPTER THREE

A NARROW PATH led from the faerie glade into the dark forest surrounding them. Roy glanced at the sky, glad to see it still touched with twilight. As long as full dark hadn't fallen, they were a safe distance from the Dark Court. Not that the Dark Realm was particularly safe.

If they needed to, they could make their way to its perilous center. But he hadn't planned to spend his evening facing off against a foe who could kill him.

That was one of the problems with being Feyguard. Injuries crossed over from the game to the real world, which meant a killing blow inflicted inside Feyland was actually deadly. All three of them had nearly died in here. And yet they kept coming back.

He shook his head, then tromped after Tam and Jennet, who had started down the trail. The sharp scent of cedar rose about him, and the crystal on Jennet's mage staff shed a soft blue light over their surroundings. Made them more visible, too, but he and Tam were both skilled fighters.

They could handle whatever they encountered—at least in this part of the realm, where elements of the game and fey world blended. Deeper in, though, Feyland truly became the Realm of Faerie, complete with treacherous and powerful magic.

The trees thinned and the path opened out into a starlit meadow, becoming a wider road. Several yards away, a small cluster of buildings huddled. Too small for a village, more likely an inn and stable for travelers, with a few scattered outbuildings and a small cottage in back for the innkeeper. No light shone in any of the windows, and the air was still. Too still.

Roy pulled his broadsword from his back. Something was in there, lurking. Waiting for them.

"Stay together," Tam said in a low voice. He, too, had drawn his sword and had his shield strapped on his left arm.

A shimmer of fire around Jennet's fingers showed that she had called up one of her spells. Slowly, they walked forward, their footsteps muffled by the dusty road. A rank odor, like tainted meat, invaded Roy's nose.

The first building they reached was a small shed. The door hung askew from only one hinge, the wood splintered and clawed. Roy tilted his blade toward the shadows inside, indicating he'd go in and check it out. Tam nodded, and Jennet raised her hands, ready to send a ball of flame into the dim recesses of the shed.

Taking shallow breaths, Roy went up to the door.

"Now," he called, flinging it open.

Jennet's fireball sizzled over his head, the orange light illuminating a heap of rags in one corner and an empty work-bench running the length of the room.

The rags stirred, first a skeletal arm emerging, then a grinning, skull-like face with leathery skin dried to the bone.

"Fresh meat," the creature said, in a creaky voice. "The master will be pleased."

"I don't think so." Roy took a firm grip on his sword.

The creature sprang forward, sunken eyes sparking with green flame, a rusty blade in its bony fingers. Roy danced back, deflecting the first strike, then sweeping his blade in a powerful, two-handed arc. The stroke cleaved the creature in two, its torso clattering to the floor while its legs remained upright.

"You all right?" Jennet called.

"Yeah. One sec." Roy stomped on the still-animate hand clawing at his leg, then lowered his sword tip to point at the creature's skull. The green sparks in its eyes were fading.

"Who is the master?" Roy asked. "What is it we face?"

"You will know… soon enough," the creature wheezed. "He has been waiting for you."

The light in its eyes winked out. With a hollow clunk, its skull separated from its spine and rolled under the bench. The hand twitching beneath Roy's foot stilled.

Dammit. He poked his sword through the empty rib cage a few times, then backed out of the shed.

"And?" Tam asked.

"A zombie-like creature who claims his master is waiting to meet us. Easy kill." Maybe too easy.

A low moan shivered through the air, making the back of Roy's neck prickle.

"Let's check out the inn," Tam said, nodding to the two-story building ahead.

"Hold up," Jennet said. "I see something."

She lowered her staff and the glowing crystal at the end dimmed and faded out. Darkness pressed against them, barely displaced by the sprinkling of stars overhead. The absence of Jennet's light revealed an eerie green glow coming from the windows of one of the rooms on the second floor, near the back corner.

"That's our target," Roy said. "Keep your staff dimmed for now. Makes us too obvious."

Moving quietly, they went to the heavy wooden door at the front of the inn. Roy pushed it open. It made a quiet squeak, but at least the hinges didn't screech terribly, like something out of a horror vid.

"Once we're inside," Tam whispered, "I'll close the door and Jennet can cast an illumination."

Roy took a few steps into the barely visible room, hoping he wouldn't stumble over a chair or empty mug. He felt Jennet behind him, and the door squeaked again as Tam came through.

A blue glow kindled from the crystal at the end of her staff, shedding light over the main room. Something skittered in the corner, long-tailed and beady-eyed. More eyes stared at them, pinpricks in the darkness.

"Rats," Tam said.

There were dozens, scavenging moldy cheese and hard bread from the tables, scurrying into the shadows.

Sword at the ready, Roy moved further into the room. He

didn't relish the idea of hacking away at the vermin. If they attacked, it wouldn't be pretty.

"Stairs on the left," Jennet said.

Her hands were again outlined in a glow—bluish white this time, denoting an arcane blast spell.

Staying close together, the three of them headed toward the stairs. The closer they got, the more the rats shifted and stared. Adrenaline pumping through him, Roy halted at the bottom of the staircase. He didn't like how the creatures were gathering. The air vibrated with the sound of their chittering.

"Get ready," he said, setting one foot on the bottom stair.

The rats came at them in a wave, a furry blanket undulating across the floor, sharp teeth bared. Jennet unleashed her arcane bolts at them, and the front wave collapsed. Their shrill cries were buried as the rest of the rats scurried over the fallen bodies.

Roy jumped down and swung his blade low, as did Tam, but melee fighters were not well suited to battling rabid rodents.

"Stand back," Jennet cried.

Flames licked about her hands, and Roy and Tam retreated to the stairs. A sheet of fire roared from Jennet across the inn, leaving the tables and benches untouched, but scorching their foes. Half the rat army fell, and the rest turned and scrambled for the shadows.

The air stank of burned hair. Hostile eyes regarded them from the edges of the room, but the rats had retreated. For now.

"Nice work," Roy said, taking shallow breaths.

"Let's get out of this stink," Tam said, starting up the stairs.

Roy let Jennet go next, then took up the rear. It made sense to keep the cloth-wearing Spellcaster between them. She could do the most damage—as she'd demonstrated below—but the tradeoff was increased personal vulnerability.

At the top of the stairs, a corridor ran the length of the inn. The room they wanted was the last door on the left, and two other doors stood open between them and their goal.

Two rooms that probably held more gruesome creatures for them to battle. They were in that strange interface between the realm and the game, which meant the battles weren't likely to be straightforward hack-n-slash. Feyland was tricky that way. Unexpected.

Magic.

As the three of them approached the first door, the room brightened, a warm golden glow spilling over the threshold. Sweet music rose, the shimmer of a harp, the plaint of bagpipes.

Roy had to fight the urge to sheathe his sword, and he could see the same struggle in Tam's set face.

"Walk past," Jennet urged as they came even with the open door.

It was a good idea—but impossible. Something wound about Roy, drawing him into the room. Tam and Jennet, too. She made a grab at the doorframe as she walked past, but the inexorable pull of the room was too strong.

"Who's there?" Tam asked into the bright fog.

Shapes moved, barely visible. High, chiming laughter mixed with the jaunty notes of the tune swirling through the air.

"I am." It was a female voice, rich with laughter and promise. "Come dance with me."

The air cleared, the brightness fading to reveal a glade of young oak trees beneath a sunset-streaked sky. Before them, a beautiful woman held out her hands. Her long golden hair fell unbound down her back, and she wore an ornate, full-skirted dress, with scarlet knotwork emblazoned on green velvet.

"I prefer not," Roy said, but his hands were already sheathing his sword.

"Such a pretty one," the faerie woman said, grasping him by the wrist. "Your blood smells so sweet."

She drew him forward, his feet going willingly, though the rest of him balked.

"Let go." He leaned away, and she tightened her grasp on his wrist.

"Oh, I think not." She turned to Tam and beckoned. "Come with me."

Eyes wide, Tam shuffled forward. Roy was dimly aware of a flurry of motion from Jennet, but with his attention magnetized to the faerie, he couldn't tell what she was doing.

The pace of the music increased. Grinning, the faerie woman danced, pulling Roy and Tam along with her.

"Stop!" Jennet cried.

A moment later, a bolt of lightning hit the faerie woman in the chest. She gasped and doubled over, and both Tam and Roy wrenched free.

Roy pulled his sword in one smooth move, and Tam did the same. The music faltered, then stopped, and the faerie woman looked up at them, her eyes now hard and glittering. She bared her sharply pointed teeth, which Roy hadn't noticed before. Beneath her green skirts, he glimpsed the cloven hooves of a goat.

"Do you deny the Glaistig?" she said, her voice no longer sweet, but full of venom.

"Afraid so," Roy said. "You're really not my type."

"Music!" she cried. "We shall dance again."

She reached for them, and Roy felt the compulsion to dance with her begin to twine about him. Beside him, he felt Tam tense. They didn't have room enough to both attack her at the same time, so he took a tiny step back, letting Tam have the first blow.

Good thing he did—Tam's slice went right through the faerie woman as if she were mist. It would have struck Roy in the side. He didn't know about friendly fire in Feyland, but suspected it would prove as dangerous as any other kind of injury.

"Arrogant mortals," the Glaistig said, her voice now whispery and dry, her form quickly fading. "You will dance with me yet."

The light faded, the grove of oak trees disappeared, and the three of them stood on the bare wooden floorboards of the inn. A dilapidated bedframe was shoved in one corner, and a stand with a cracked washbasin occupied the other. Except for that, the room was empty.

"Let's go," Tam said.

The greasy feel of the Glaistig's grasp still coated Roy's palm. When they got out of the room, he held his sword one-handed and wiped his fingers against the leather strap of his armor.

"How did you keep your wits in there?" he asked, turning to Jennet. She looked different, her robes rumpled.

"As soon as the faerie's attention focused on you two, I turned my clothing inside out," she said. "It's a trick Tam and I used once before to deflect the attention of the fey folk."

"Easy for you to do." Roy glanced down at the straps and greaves of his armor.

"Well, yeah." She smiled at him. "Somebody had to act, and you two seemed… occupied."

Tam frowned. Roy suspected it was because his girlfriend had just gotten undressed in front of another guy—not that Roy had noticed.

"Also," Jennet said, "the Glaistig was focusing on you two a lot more. Probably because you're guys."

"Cute guys," Roy said, winking.

"Right." Jennet rolled her eyes.

"Let's get going," Tam said. "There's another room to clear before we hit the final door."

When they were still a few paces from the next door, a gang of twig-limbed creatures leaped out. They brandished spears and scythes, their grins as wickedly sharp as their weapons.

Roy quickly tallied them up. Seven against three. Not great odds, but not terrible. And easier to deal with than the Glaistig in the last room. He preferred the straightforward fights.

"Sending in Wall of Flame," Jennet said, before he and Tam could charge forward.

Orange fire rippled down the hallway, and two of the creatures shrieked as they caught fire. Their companions beat out the flames, and as a unit, they charged.

Tam took the lead, shield raised to deflect the spear points. Roy swung his broadsword in a strong arc, and one of the attackers collapsed into a gangly pile of sticks.

One of Jennet's blue magebolts sizzled past his shoulder, catching another of the creatures squarely in the chest. Tam ran a third through with his sword, sending more twigs flying. The odds were looking better all the time.

Until the piles of twiggy limbs twitched and shuddered, and then somehow coalesced into a single creature, much larger than the remaining four. His scythe had grown too, and Roy felt uncomfortably like a stalk of wheat.

"Duck!" Tam yelled as the creature swung, the huge blade whistling overhead.

Roy crouched, then sprang up again, fending off two of the smaller attackers, while Tam engaged the other two. Jennet sent another bolt of magic at the big creature, which only seemed to anger it.

No time for finesse. Roy swept his blade through his two adversaries, who clattered to the floor into bundles of twitching twigs.

"Burn them," he called to Jennet.

She ignited the piles, then sent flames at the ones Tam had just taken down, too.

The large creature howled and surged forward to stomp on the piles. The flames died, and the twigs incorporated into the enemy. Its head now brushed the tall ceiling, its shoulders nearly blocking the hallway.

"Great." Roy traded a look with Tam.

Instead of seven stick figures, they faced a giant, scythe-wielding twig creature with seemingly limitless powers of regeneration. He never thought he'd find branches quite so... menacing. Blind eyes made of twisted whorls of wood stared at them. Blind, but not sightless, as the huge, curved blade sheering toward them proved.

Tam brought his shield up to block the blow, and Roy braced his sword, too. With an ear-shattering clang, the scythe bit into the shield. Tam swayed, but stood fast, while Roy felt the shock all the way down to his feet.

"Next time, we duck," he said, the words buzzing in his ears.

While the creature was distracted with them, Jennet blasted another fireball, hitting it in the leg. A tendril of smoke arose, but their enemy brushed at the flame, like brushing dust off a coat. The fire died.

They were in deep trouble.

"Um, guys?" Jennet's voice sounded strained. "Don't look now, but the rats have all come up the stairs. Even the ones we killed."

"Zombie rats," Roy said. "Our day can't get any better, can it?"

Now that Jennet mentioned it, he could hear the scritch of claws coming down the hallway. Before he could take a quick look behind him, the twig giant swept at them again with its scythe. This time, both he and Tam leaped away from the sharp blade.

"Follow me!" Tam cried. "Back into the empty room."

Roy nodded. It would be easier to defend, and he didn't think their huge opponent could fit through the door. He hoped.

The three of them fell back, the twig creature closing in on one side, the rats on the other. As Roy had guessed, the giant couldn't fit through the door. It poked at them with its scythe, but the attacks were limited.

However, the rats came through with no problem.

"Move to the left side of the room," Jennet called as the furry—and boney, and bloody—wave poured in.

Roy kicked at the rodents swarming him. Tam did the same, and Jennet raised her staff.

"I'm going to summon Wall of Flame again," she gasped, running back and forth to keep away from the rats. "Get ready to dash through it to the other side."

"Good plan," Tam said. "Hurry."

She kindled a sheet of fire, bisecting the room, and the three of them ran across it. Roy felt a faint tingling across his skin, but the magic seemed to know he wasn't an enemy. The rats drew up short, squealing, even the dead ones.

"That won't hold them long," he said.

"Back out in the hallway," Tam said. "Last I checked, rats weren't good at opening doors."

Jennet nodded, her face pale with the effort of sustaining her flames. Usually her fire just swept through and was gone.

The twig giant roared and poked his scythe into the room again.

"Now!" Tam yelled, ducking under the blade.

Roy and Jennet followed on his heels. But they couldn't shut the door with the handle of the scythe in the way. A few of the braver rats jumped the fire and scurried toward them, sharp teeth bared and eyes glinting. The rest would surely follow.

"Hey, ugly," Tam called, darting down the hall and waving his sword at the twig creature.

It roared and pulled its weapon from the doorway. Roy slammed the heavy wooden door closed, just as the first rats reached it. It wouldn't hold them back forever, but they didn't need that long.

Tam had backed down the hall almost to the stairs, keeping the twig giant focused on him. Its wide back made a tempting target. Through the cage of its branch-woven ribs, Roy glimpsed something round and fleshy, like a fungus growing out of rotten wood. It moved, pulsing in a slow rhythm.

"Look," he said to Jennet, his voice low. "See its heart?"

She nodded. "That's our target."

They charged forward, Jennet's fingers flickering with arcane energy, Roy's sword raised. He aimed for a thin opening between the branches, putting all his strength into the blow. Blue-white magic hit at the same time, and from the other direction, Tam's sword pierced the creature.

It screeched, the sound like branches scraping against a window, then lurched forward. Tam darted out of the way, surprisingly nimble for a guy dressed all in silver armor.

The screeching quieted, becoming the gust of wind in the trees as the twig giant slowly collapsed. Branches rained down, scatterings of kindling and moss. The two heavy eye-whorls thumped to the wooden floorboards, and the scythe clattered against the wall.

Tam circled around to join them, and the three of them warily backed down the hall.

"Is it defeated?" Jennet asked.

"Maybe." Tam kept his sword and shield at the ready. "Or maybe not."

Roy was pretty sure the twig giant was down, but it was better not to take chances in Feyland.

"Burn it?" he asked.

"Yes." Jennet sent a bright orange fireball streaking down the hall.

It hit the branches and continued to burn. Nothing put the flames out, and soon the air was filled with smoke and the crackle of fire consuming wood.

"Time for the last door," Tam said. "Before the inn catches fire."

As they passed the closed first door, Roy heard the thumps of bodies flinging themselves against the wood, and furious gnawing. Those rats wanted out.

Fire on one side, zombie rodents on the other. Great. He could hardly wait to see what awaited behind the final door.

CHAPTER FOUR

THE DOOR at the end of the corridor creaked wider. Eerie green light spilled across the threshold, as if whatever waited for them grew impatient. The hallway filled with smoke, and the angry squeals of half-dead rats.

Roy, Tam, and Jennet hastened the last few paces down the hall. The green glow tarnished Tam's armor with verdigris, and made Jennet's pale complexion look sickly. Roy glanced at his own armor, seeing it had turned a moldy yellowish color.

Behind them, the fire crackled and the rats thudded against the door down the hall.

Tam's face was grim, and Roy felt the same. Shoulder to shoulder, weapons at the ready, the two of them strode up to the threshold.

And froze.

"Oh, crap," Roy said under his breath.

In the middle of the glowing room stood a figure encased in black armor—except for his head. Half of his helm was missing, revealing a skull-like face. The single visible eye stared at them, lit with sparks of malicious green. His jaw line was partially rotted away, stretched into the parody of a leering grin.

Behind them, Jennet let out a strangled gasp.

"The Black Knight." Tam said the words like a curse, which they basically were.

So much for defeating the knight in their epic battle against the Dark Queen. He was back, and apparently worse than ever.

"We meet again, mortals," the knight said. His voice echoed hollowly. "Do come in. I have a score to settle with you."

"Likewise," Roy said. He clutched the pommel of his sword hard between his hands.

"You." The Black Knight leaned forward, and cold air scented with decay wafted over them. "You still live, while I am trapped mid-existence, in agony, to serve my queen."

"Killing us isn't going to give you your life back," Tam said.

He stepped into the room. Roy followed, moving a few paces away so they'd have space to fight. Jennet slipped in behind them, keeping the wall at her back.

"No." The knight lifted his black sword. "But your deaths will bring me much satisfaction, and make this so-called living bearable for a time."

The knight rushed forward, and Tam barely got his shield up in time. The clang of black blade on silver metal was like a harsh bell. Roy stabbed at the knight, but the enemy was too quick, swiveling with superhuman speed to block his blow, then aiming a slashing counterattack at Roy's head.

He ducked back, and Tam moved in for another strike.

Blue-white magic splattered against the knight's dark helm, and he grinned, jaw gaping.

"Your magic has little effect on me, Fair Jennet. I have been tempered by the fires of death."

Roy heard her curse under her breath. If the Black Knight was now immune to magic, her Spellcaster wasn't going to do much good.

Tam whacked at the knight's arm, and their enemy responded by pressing the attack. The tip of his black sword nicked Tam's shoulder, sliding between the armor joints, and Tam scrambled back, face twisted in pain.

Yelling, Roy rushed forward, buying Tam time to recover. Adrenaline beat in his veins, hot and heady. He landed a fierce two-handed blow on the knight's chest, denting his armor, then spun away. A gout of magical fire hit where Roy had just struck, then sprayed harmlessly off. Jennet would keep trying, and at the very least her attacks would distract the knight, even if they did no damage.

Tam worked his way around to the other side of their enemy, but damn if the knight didn't move faster than they could track, his defensive moves blurring back and forth, punctuated by sharp stabs and slices from his deadly black blade.

Still, the knight didn't manage to land any more blows. Sweat trickled down the back of Roy's neck. The fight was quickly becoming a stalemate. Although the Black Knight would probably be able to outlast them, given that he was a magical, partially dead creature. Which meant they needed to end the fight, soon.

From the corner of his eye, he caught a blur of blue. What was Jennet doing now?

He glanced at her, and it nearly cost him a hand as the knight's blade sliced down. Roy leaped back, desperately sweeping his sword up. The echo of the blow rang through his blade and jarred his wrists and forearms. He'd seen enough to make him bare his teeth in a grin, though.

The Black Knight might ignore Jennet, but that didn't mean she couldn't contribute to the fight. She was kneeling, holding her staff parallel to the ground, eyes fixed on the fight.

"Now!" Tam yelled, clearly aware of what she intended.

Jennet swept her staff out, catching their enemy across one ankle as he pivoted. The sturdy wood tangled his feet for just long enough that Tam body-slammed the knight.

The two of them went down, but Roy was ready. As soon as their opponent hit the floor, he thrust his sword through the Black Knight's chest, putting all his strength behind the blow.

The blade passed through darkness and the point stuck, hard, into the wooden floor. The Black Knight was gone, his body turned to smoke and shadows.

"You will not defeat me so easily." The knight's deep, disembodied voice resonated through the room. "We shall meet again, foolish mortals."

A chilly wind gusted through the door, and the knight's presence faded.

"Dammit." Tam rose, wincing as he moved his right arm.

Grimly, Roy yanked at his sword. On the third tug, he

managed to wrench it free of the floorboards. The shining length of the blade gleamed, the edges nicked from battle.

Jennet's face was pale. "We need to log off, and see how badly Tam's hurt."

"I'm fine."

"Don't play the hero," Roy said. "Jennet's right—and besides, it's not like we can pursue the knight."

"Unless we go all the way to the Dark Court." Jennet gave a little shudder.

Tam lifted his head. "I smell smoke—and rats. Let's get out of here."

Roy didn't need any convincing.

A few moments later, he lifted off the gaming helmet. The swirling in his stomach could be ignored—and he'd have the staff bring some fruit juice and rolls. Eating something helped tamp down the disorientation from crossing over to the realm.

Jennet sat up in her chair and stripped off her gaming gloves. "At least we know the gateway is still intact. Nothing's coming through that way."

"There are other ways," Tam said grimly. "Could you help with my helmet and gloves?"

While Jennet assisted Tam, Roy opened the first-aid station in the wall. Since the first injury carryover from Feyland, he kept it stocked with disinfectant, bandages, and plas-skin.

"Doesn't look too bad," he said, once Jennet helped Tam remove his T-shirt.

The cut wasn't too deep, but it was long, and oozed a sluggish trickle of blood. Jennet grabbed the supplies out of Roy's hands and went into doctor mode.

"Bad news, that the Black Knight is still alive," Tam said.

"Or some semblance of alive," Roy said. "What do we do now? Check the Bright Court for leakage?"

"Attention," the house announced. "Dr. Lassiter is returning home. Dinner will be served in forty minutes."

"We obviously can't go in right now," Jennet said. "How about tomorrow afternoon?"

"I can't miss my internship hours," Tam said. "Some of the VirtuMax employees are just waiting for me to screw up so they can boot me out."

"You know you have my dad's support." Jennet sprayed plas-skin over Tam's cut.

"Yeah, but there are plenty of other folks who'd like to see the Exie out on his ass."

Roy folded his arms. He had the uncomfortable feeling his mom was one of those people. That was, if she even bothered to think about it from her lofty CEO office.

"I'll check out the Bright Court later tonight," Roy said. "It's not nearly as dangerous on that side."

"You shouldn't enter game alone," Jennet said.

Her concern warmed Roy. Having friends—real ones, not just followers—was a feeling he was getting used to.

"Actually, of all of us I'll probably have the best reception from the king. If we go together, he might get a bit... defensive."

"I agree," Tam said. "And I don't want you anywhere near that guy, Jennet. Roy can do it."

"All right," she said, giving Roy a pointed look. "Be careful, though, and let us know when you go in. We don't want to have to haul you out, like last time."

"I can handle it." He hoped. Though he and the Bright King hadn't parted on the best of terms, Roy had done him a few favors. Things like that carried weight with the fey folk—even if it was stuff that Roy wasn't proud of doing. All the more reason to use it as leverage.

After Tam and Jennet left, Roy headed to his room, a strange restlessness running just beneath his skin. For some reason, he couldn't get Brea's face out of his mind. Frowning, he grabbed his tablet and opened the art suite. It was one of the only things he kept encrypted. Not that he was a great artist or anything, but his sketches weren't that bad.

Drawing was often the only way he could ease his mood. Not that he was all emo and about to start wearing black and painting his nails. Nobody knew he drew stuff—except his mom, who years ago had deleted his first attempts and told him to stop daydreaming.

For a while, he had.

But ever since encountering the Realm of Faerie, ideas and images itched inside his head, burned his fingers until he managed to get them out.

He'd watched a bunch of tutorials and figured out the basics of shadow and texture, but the things he envisioned weren't easy to capture. At least, not with the tools he had. What he really needed was a high-end graphics manipulation program.

And maybe even some old-school art supplies. Canvas, paint, things like that. Of course, it would be impossible to hide that stuff from his mom. He could amass all the gaming and tech equip he wanted, but she'd made it clear that there was no place in his life for art.

He'd better stick with digital painting on his tablet for now. He could tell her he wanted to do some game design work. As long as there was a "practical" application, she'd have no problem buying the programs for him. In the meantime, he'd work with what he had—a basic art platform with stripped-down features.

He put his tablet on the desk stand and hooked it to the pen pad, then picked up the stylus and began to draw.

Half an hour later, he sat back and squinted at his screen. A maiden looked back at him, her dark hair tangled with white flowers, her eyes touched with wildness. It wasn't quite Brea, but close—and the itch in his head had calmed enough that he could hear himself think.

"Please prepare to dine," the house said. "The appetizer course will be served in five minutes."

"Right," Roy said. "On my way."

He ran the glitter brush around the edges of Brea's hair one more time. He hadn't gotten her nose right. Tomorrow, in PreCalc, he'd make a couple quick sketches when she wasn't looking.

CHAPTER FIVE

AFTER DINNER—WHICH was boring as usual due to his mom spending most of it interfacing on her tablet and messager—Roy headed to the game theater. Time to check out the Bright Court.

He fired up the FullD. Before donning his sim gear, he sent Jennet a quick message, letting her know he was logging in to Feyland, and that he'd be in touch if he found anything.

:Go easy,: she sent back.

:Will do.:

He signed off, then slipped into the sim chair and pulled on his gloves. Despite his assurances to his friends, his palms were sweaty with nerves. Still, he was the best guy for the job.

At the avatar selection screen, he paused. Probably he should take in his Mercenary, but going alone into the Bright Court as that character left a bitter taste on his tongue. Too many echoes of when he'd first played Feyland, and had found himself in a magical—and astonishingly real—realm. At first he'd been exhilarated and overwhelmed, especially when the king had offered him the power to make all his dreams come true.

The price hadn't seemed so bad, at the time. Help siphon energy from the real world to the Realm of Faerie, to help them survive—no problem. Looking back, Roy could trace his steps down the path of bad choices. He'd helped the king, transferring more and more mortal essence into the realm, and causing true harm to his victims. His own arrogance had blinded him to the cost. And the emptiness he'd felt inside hadn't really been filled by making everyone at Crestview High adore him.

But at least the Bright King hadn't marked him for human sacrifice the way the Dark Queen had done to both Jennet and Tam.

Shaking off the memories, he chose his alternate character of the Illuminer. His avatar wore a golden robe over basic trousers and jerkin. Despite the fact he was a magic user, he carried a dagger sheathed at his belt.

Always good to have a weapon handy.

He lifted his finger in the command to enter Feyland, concentrated on reaching the gateway, then gritted his teeth as the nauseating swirl of golden light encircled him. When it cleared, he stood in the center faerie ring, a mix of pale mushrooms and white-speckled ones surrounding him.

Roy sent a glance toward the shadowed glade leading to the Dark Realm, then strode over to the sunshine-filled one. First, he inspected the boundary. The line of salt the Feyguard had laid remained unbroken.

He pushed through the wall, into the Bright Realm's clearing. Sunshine warmed the top of his head, and birdsong filled the air. The bright sparkle of pixies flashed in the branches of the silver-leafed trees.

There was no definite sign that some creature had managed to pass into the mortal world. Most importantly, there were no guards, no masses of elfin knights, no bright-eyed sprites—nothing to suggest the realm's denizens were planning an assault.

That wasn't proof of anything, though. He'd need to get to the court and talk to the king. Once, he'd had a shortcut that took him directly to the center of the Bright Realm. Did it still work?

Closing his eyes, he turned three times around, going counterclockwise, and said the rhyme the king had given him.

"Widdershins, I chant and sing,

Thrice about the faerie ring,

Take me now to see the king!"

Even through his closed lids, Roy sensed the flash of yellow light engulfing him. When it faded, he carefully opened his eyes. He stood in a glade of copper-trunked trees, their leaves made of jade and emerald, bright gems of flowers winking from the upper branches. Sweet chiming filled the air, and the strains of a Celtic harp playing a lively jig.

A relieved breath escaped Roy's lips. He'd made it, without having to battle and quest through the entire Bright Realm. Of course, one look at him and the king might throw him out on his ass.

He glanced up, marking the direction of the enormous, glowing ruby that illuminated the court like a miniature sun, then headed that direction. Sooner than he might have wished, he reached the brilliant clearing of the Bright Court.

As he stepped onto the lush green grass, the harp music faded. Seven bright pixies flashed toward him, zooming about his head and crying out in their high-pitched language. The faerie maidens and elfin knights arrayed on silk-draped couches looked up, their eyes full of immortal secrets.

At the center of the court, the king sat on his golden throne. His sharp-planed, handsome face regarded Roy impassively, his eyes hard as sapphires.

"Your majesty." Roy took three steps toward the throne, then knelt and bent his head. Didn't hurt to show some respect.

"Royal One." The king's voice was sonorous, and Roy winced at his old name.

When the creatures of Feyland had started calling him that, he'd considered it his due. Not only was it his name, he was the heir to the power and fortunes of the Lassiters, and reveled in his status. Now, though, he'd be happier without that weight.

"Forgive the intrusion," Roy said.

He made himself glance up, though the king was more impressive and frightening than Roy recalled. Or maybe he'd just been stupider and more arrogant, unable to see the force of magic shining from the monarch.

The king leaned forward, steepling his long, pale fingers. "I had not thought to see you again, mortal—and certainly not in the center of my court. What is afoot that brings such an unexpected, and perhaps foolish, visitor to my court?"

Though the king's voice was mild, Roy heard the threat in his words.

"I wish to know if any of your subjects have entered the

mortal world recently." Roy glanced about the court, but he had no way of telling if any of the various creatures were missing.

"And what price will you pay for the answer?" the king asked, his eyes gleaming.

"A fair one, for the truth." Hopefully, it was the right thing to say. The fey folk were always trying to be sly, and Roy hoped he hadn't just fallen into some kind of trap.

The pixies chimed with laughter overhead, and the king nodded.

"Well spoken," he said. "Rise, mortal. I see you have changed your demeanor from warrior to scribe. It is a fitting choice."

"Um, okay." Roy got to his feet and carefully approached the king. He wasn't quite sure what the king meant by that remark, but it didn't seem too negative.

"Give me your hand. For the time it takes me to speak the answer to your question, I shall pull forth your mortal essence."

"That doesn't seem like a good idea."

The king smiled, and it was not a reassuring sight. "Fair price for fair answers, Royal One. Or shall I send you back to the mortal world with the question still weighing?"

"Fine." Throat dry, Roy extended his hand.

The Bright King set two fingers on the back of his hand, and Roy braced himself. Damn, he hoped he could walk out under his own power after this.

"The answer is no," the king said. "No creature of the Bright Court has entered the mortal realm for over a century."

A wave of dizziness swept over Roy. He blinked, hard, as

the king lifted his fingers. The radiance surrounding the throne was now so bright Roy had to squint to see through it.

"What about Puck?" he asked.

The pixies chimed again, and the king flashed a smile. "Puck is a creature of the realm entire. Neither court claims him—or would want to."

The elfin maids and knights laughed at this, the sound so musical and sweet it made Roy's knees weak. Or maybe that was the effect of the king's touch.

"Go now, mortal. You have your answer—now trouble me no more."

The Bright King waved his hand, and Roy braced himself. Sure enough, the sickening golden light swirled about him, marking his transition back into the real world.

A second later he sat in his sim chair, his stomach churning, sweat dampening his scalp. He felt like he'd just run a virtual marathon while suffering from food poisoning. After a few deep breaths, he levered himself up and peeled off his sim gear.

His messager blinked urgently from the seat of the FullD beside him. Roy fumbled to reach it, and peered at the screen. A message from Jennet, of course.

:You out yet? Everything all right?:

:All clear,: he managed.

:You ok?!:

:Good enuf. Srsly.:

:I can come over if you need help.:

:No.: Already he was feeling a little stronger. *:Tell you guys tomorrow, but nothing came through from Bright Court.:*

:All right, if you're sure. Good night.:

:Night.:

He shut off his messager and levered himself out of the sim chair. The room wavered a little, but he figured he could make it up to his room, drink a gallon of water, and pass out for the night.

CHAPTER SIX

Brea slipped through the current of students flowing through Crestview High's halls. That morning, she'd arrived at the beginning of the school day and positioned herself in the lower hallway. Her fingers tingling lightly with magic, she moved from person to person, brushing each one unobtrusively in passing.

It wasn't always possible to touch their skin directly. She had to content herself with a momentary press of her hand against a shoulder, a quick grasp at the edge of a coat, and hope the magic would seep in far enough to do its job.

She'd only marked a handful of the humans before her breath began coming too quickly, a haze of dizziness falling before her eyes. She had the strength for one more before she must stop and regather her powers. Oh, the queen would be angry—but then, she should not have sent such a small denizen of the realm to undertake this work in the mortal world.

Brea's magic was made of ripple and starlight, depleted too

soon on even small castings. It would be another few turning of days before she was sufficiently recovered to resume her mission.

A girl with long blonde hair walked past, and Brea reached, letting magic spill from her fingers into the wayward strands of hair.

"Hey!" The girl whirled, one hand going to her head. "What are you doing?"

Brea shrank back. She was weary, and had carelessly pulled the girl's hair.

"I beg your pardon," she said.

The blonde girl's expression sharpened, her pale blue eyes suddenly full of too much interest. "Are you that Irish girl?"

Who had been talking of her? Brea's heartbeat quickened, and her gaze went to the edges of the hall, seeking shadows where she might hide.

"I'm Jennet," the girl said.

"Brea." She offered no more.

They stood in a little eddy of quiet. The other students hurried past, parting around them as if they were two stones in the stream.

"Hm." Jennet's gaze was too piercing, as if she could see through Brea's human façade to the creature beneath. "Well, Brea, come join me and my friends at lunch. We'll be at the table near the back."

"You are too kind." It was not an acceptance, nor a thank-you.

Jennet opened her mouth, and the blare of the bell cut through the air, halting whatever words she had been about to speak. Brea had not thought she would ever welcome that horrid, mechanical sound, but at that moment she did.

"I must find my class." She quickly turned before the girl could offer help.

Though the effort left her shaking, she drew a hasty masking spell over herself as she darted down the hall, away from Jennet's too-knowing gaze.

There was no danger... and yet Brea was in this very city because humans had crossed over into the realm here, numerous times before. The pattern of possibilities was strong in this place, and easier to shape to the queen's wishes.

Still, Brea would be wise to sink below the surface for a time. When she emerged again, she must take better care.

She let out a quiet breath, a sigh that would be a melancholy song in her world. Home was still so very far away, and she had much to accomplish before the queen allowed her to return.

———

"I think I met your Irish girl," Jennet said to Roy when he plopped his lunch tray down on their table.

"You don't know?"

"Not exactly." Jennet pressed her lips together. "She did say her name was Brea, but I couldn't get anything else out of her. I invited her to join us for lunch. Somehow, I don't think she'll show. She seemed nervous."

"Hey," Marny said. "She's a new student in a foreign school. You'd be nervous, too."

"It was more than that. There was something fey about her."

Tam sat up straight and pushed his hair out of his eyes. "Roy, do you agree?"

"Maybe. I'll check her out in math class this afternoon."

Marny snorted. "Of course you will. Jennet, stop kicking me."

"Give Roy some credit."

"Yeah." Roy raised one eyebrow—a move he'd spent weeks perfecting when he was twelve. "I can be subtle."

"Right." Marny rolled her eyes, but a smile lurked at the corners of her mouth.

One of her favorite hobbies was tweaking him. Not that he didn't deserve it, especially in the past. But he was changing. Which was damn uncomfortable, though not without its rewards, like having real friends that gave him a hard time.

He was completely prepped to be smooth, yet thorough, by the time math class rolled around. The only problem was, Brea wasn't in class.

Well, that wasn't the only problem. A chorus of groans filled the air as his classmates entered the room and saw the pop quizzes waiting on each table. Mr. Brinksea had just finished distributing them to the back of the room.

"No quiz for the new girl?" Roy asked, indicating the bare space on the table beside him.

Mr. Brinksea blinked at him. "If you're trying to score a copy to smuggle out of my class, Lassiter, you'll have to do better than that."

"What? No—I mean the new student who joined the class yesterday."

"What are you talking about?"

Unease shivered through Roy. "Brea Cairgead. Exchange student, with long, dark hair. You don't remember her?"

"Lassiter, I recommend you drop this weak attempt at pranking me. It's amusing no one." Mr. Brinksea raised his voice. "Class, this will be a dark-tablet test. Work quietly. Once you finish, bring your quiz to me. When the bell rings, begin."

Swallowing back his frustration, Roy pulled the paper toward him. Mr. Brinksea's eyes had been absolutely clear and truthful. The teacher had no memory of Brea Cairgead attending his class.

"Pst, Jonez." Roy reached over and tagged the student sitting in front of him.

"I am not helping you cheat on this," the dark-haired boy said, "so don't even ask."

"I could ace this in my sleep, man. No—do you remember a girl sitting here yesterday, beside me?"

Jonez shook his head. "Quit talking to me, or Brinksea will fail both of us."

Roy scooted back into his chair and resisted the urge to chew on his stylus. Something freaky was going on with Brea. She was too conveniently absent for it to be a coincidence.

CHAPTER SEVEN

THE MOON CHASED the sun across the sky a handful of times before Brea unwound herself from her dreams of spider silk and moonbeams. No one had disturbed her enchanted sleep as she rested upon her velvet coverlet. The dilapidated walls of her shelter were bespelled with aversions, so that no one would desire to enter. She had placed extra protections around the gaping doorway, the broken windows, and the ragged holes in the roof.

True, she might have chosen a different place, but the permanence of human buildings disturbed her; the rough order they tried to impose on a world that should be free. The decay of the Exe crept slowly forward, and she found comfort in the tumbledown shelter, and the fact she could see the light and feel the wind, even inside her poor dwelling.

Despite the putrid stench in the night air, she took a deep breath and smiled up at the orange city-glow washing the stars to dimness. She felt much restored.

A pinprick of light appeared in the middle of her shelter,

quickly expanding into a glowing sphere. The chiming enchantment of the Realm of Faerie filled the air. Heart pattering, Brea backed toward the crumbling wall. She summoned her magic, so newly regained. It might be a friend who stepped forth from the bright portal, but 'twas far more likely to be a foe.

Guiltily, she glanced about her shelter. She had appropriated softness and brightness from the human world—pillows filled with feathers, a string of crystals that sparkled in the sun, a silken velvet coverlet in deep sapphire for her bed. It was comfortable. Too comfortable, perchance, for one supposed to be cast into the cold mortal realm to tirelessly do the queen's bidding.

But there was nothing to be done now, except wait.

She held her breath as a figure formed in the center of the light—a long-fingered creature, capering as it approached. With an audible pop, as of a bubble bursting, the creature arrived in the mortal world.

"Puck." Relief coursed through her like sweet water as she recognized those bright eyes beneath a wild tangle of hair.

"Maid Brea." The sprite hovered in midair and made her a jaunty bow. "I trust I find you well?"

"Well enough."

Despite her gladness to see him, and the pleasure of catching a faint breath of the wild air of the realm, she was cautious. Puck did the queen's bidding—when it suited him. Other times, he was as feckless as a bit of thistledown borne by the whims of the wind and subject to no rule but his own.

"How fares your quest here?" Puck asked. "The queen is eager to witness your success."

Brea wove her fingers together. "Marking the humans wearies me more than I expected. I have touched but few, and I know not whether that is sufficient. My powers are too quickly depleted."

"Unfortunate." Puck settled cross-legged, still floating. "The queen will not be pleased to learn of this. She was expecting more."

He waved his hand, the gesture followed by a glittering trail of dust. It slowly filtered down to settle on the cracked cement floor in a swirl faint as starlight. Brea studied it, and frowned.

"If the queen is displeased, then she ought to have sent a more powerful agent," she said. "I am but a small creature of the realm, and my magics are not great."

"You were the only one who could pass through," Puck said. "A flawed tool is better than none. But I must return to the queen with more fruitful tidings than this. Tell me of the mortals you've encountered."

"There is little to tell." Brea feigned a laugh. "They are easily led to see what their own minds believe, and they are all foolish."

Puck leaped to his feet and turned a flip, ending up staring directly into her eyes. "Take care. Not all humans are as blind as you might imagine."

She blinked, thinking uneasily of Roy Lassiter and the pale-haired girl she had touched in the halls. It would not do to discount Puck's warning. Yet she was reluctant to speak of them, to let the sprite carry tales of her failures back to the queen.

"I will do what I may," she said.

"And do you still have the medallion, safe and secure?"

She glanced at the small wooden chest, banded with bronze, that sat in the corner. It glowed softly with enchantments—spells of concealment and binding. Within lay the means to step once more between the worlds, and return to the realm. But only once she had done the Dark Queen's bidding.

Until that time, the silver-runed medallion must remain nestled away.

"Aye," she said. "I know well how precious and powerful it is."

"Guard it well. Should such a thing fall into the wrong hands, mayhem would follow." Puck sounded more serious than she would ever have expected from such a merry creature. "I shall return anon, to hear more of your progress."

He lifted his fingers to his head in a formal salute. Then, between one fluttering heartbeat and the next, he was gone. The magic he had scattered upon the floor faded, and her shelter seemed dim and poor. Brea hugged her arms about herself, feeling suddenly small and alone, and no match for the human world.

CHAPTER EIGHT

"How can a student just disappear for a week?" Roy asked at lunch.

"Maybe she's had the flu," Marny said, but Tam shook his head.

"I didn't imagine her." Roy knew his voice had a defensive edge, but he couldn't help himself.

"I saw her, too." Jennet patted his arm. "She'll be back. Keep your eyes open."

"I'm not so sure an ultra-nervous foreign exchange student is the best match for Roy," Marny said. "He's only going to scare her off."

"Because I'm so prime?" he asked, mostly to distract himself and get a reaction.

Marny rolled her eyes. "So tweaked, you mean."

"Hold up," Tam said. "She's here."

"Seriously? Where?" Roy sat up and started scanning the cafeteria.

"Way to be obvious," Marny said. "Why not jump up on the table and yell her name while you're at it?"

Roy slouched a little, but didn't stop looking. He needed to at least catch a glimpse of Brea. None of his sketches had turned out right.

"Back corner," Tam said.

"Hm." Jennet narrowed her eyes. "She's doing a good job of not being noticed."

Roy followed her gaze. Sure enough, Brea sat at the very end of a table in the far corner. A light was burned out there, and her dark hair and gray sweater blended with the shadows.

"I'm going over to talk to her," Roy said.

"Go slow," Tam said. "There's something odd about that girl."

Roy nodded and grabbed the leather strap of his pack. "See you guys after school."

Despite what Marny thought, he wasn't going to charge up and park himself in front of Brea. Instead, he cut around to the side, deliberately keeping out of her sight. The other students at the tables barely glanced up as he went by.

Three tables away, then two. So far, Brea hadn't noticed him.

Holding back a grin of triumph, Roy slid onto the bench across from her.

"Hey there," he said.

She gave him a wide-eyed, startled look, and began to rise.

"Wait." He reached and set his hand on her arm.

The touch sent a spark through him, something quick and unexpected. She froze, then slowly sat back down again. Roy lifted his hand, resisting the urge to stare at his palm. He had the feeling that if he took his eyes off Brea, she would disappear.

"Hello," she said, her voice breathless.

"I haven't seen you around for a few days," he said. "Where've you been?"

"An illness fell over me, and I retreated to rest and regain my strength."

It was a weird way of saying she'd been sick—but then, she was from a foreign country.

"I hope you're feeling better. You missed a quiz in PreCalc."

"Oh." She blushed, the color high on her pale cheeks, and dropped her gaze to the table. "I am no longer enrolled in that mathematics class."

Disappointment pulled Roy's stomach down. "So I guess we don't have any classes together."

"I suppose not." She did not lift her eyes.

"Listen. You're new here. Let me show you around Crestview. Not that there's a lot to see and do, but still."

He wasn't sure where the impulse came from to ask her out, but he trusted it. Sure, he thought Brea was cute, in a delicate kind of way—but it was more than that.

"I..." She glanced up then, her eyes wide and a little afraid.

"You don't have to be alone with me," Roy hurried to add. "I bet my friends would join us. We can go someplace public. I want you to feel safe."

Something flashed in Brea's gaze, silvery and elusive. Then, slowly, she nodded.

"Perhaps it would be good, to spend time with a small

handful of people. I feel a bit lost here." She looked across the cafeteria, something bewildered in her face.

He smiled at her, hoping to spark an answering expression. So far, he wasn't sure she knew how to smile. "Are you free after school today?"

"Yes." Her shoulders curved forward, as if she regretted saying the word.

"Then meet us out front." He paused, studying her nose. It was a bit smaller and sharper than he'd been drawing. "Will you be there?"

"I will." Her lips stayed in a straight, unsmiling line.

The sound of the bell cut harshly though the air, and Brea rose, her movements quick and fluid.

"See you later," Roy said.

She nodded, then hurried away. Her long, dark hair was pulled back into a braid reaching nearly to her waist. The cafeteria lights gave it an odd, silvery sheen.

What a skittish thing she was. He didn't like to speculate about people's pasts, but there was something in Brea's behavior that made him wonder. Orphan? Abusive family?

Or had his first instinct been correct, and she'd been somehow touched by the fey folk?

Although that was a tricky subject to broach. *Hey there, did you accidentally stumble into the Realm of Faerie at some point?* No —he'd need to get to know her better before asking questions that would make her think he was insane.

Whatever it was with her, he'd go slow. At least he'd made some progress. As long as his friends didn't frighten her off, he might eventually end up on a real date with Brea, and get a start on figuring out her secrets.

Brea sat in the back of English class, letting the teacher's voice wash over her. They were studying James Joyce. Secret amusement warmed her. That man had spent more than a passing amount of time in the Realm of Faerie, though she'd never actually met him. Lower denizens such as herself did not mix with the members of the courts.

Unless forced to. She pushed away the memory of her transformation, the terrifying interview before the Dark Queen, and the subsequent, impossible, task laid upon her.

Meeting Roy and his friends after school might ease her burden. Instead of trying to imbue dozens of passing mortals with fey magic, perhaps she could infect a small handful, over time. It certainly would be less taxing on her small store of power. And give her a greater chance of success, thereby deflecting the queen's wrath.

Not that it would be a simple thing, to spend so much time in the close presence of mortals. Still, she must do what her mission required.

When the last bell rang, cawing like a raucous metal crow, Brea gathered her courage in both hands. Rather than fading into the shadows and fleeing to her bolt-hole in the Exe, she stepped through the doors of Crestview High into the warm spring sunlight.

Roy was already outside, waiting on the struggling patch of greenery. His friends stood with him: another boy, a big, dark-haired girl, and...

Brea halted at the sight of the blonde girl she had met in the hallway during her first, ill-fated attempt at sowing magic.

Fear prickled down her arms. She was about to back away and run into the school, when Roy noticed her.

"Brea!" he called, waving.

Too late to retreat. She took a moment to try and still her trembling heart, then walked forward. The blonde girl—Jennet, as she recalled—watched Brea, her eyes full of questions.

"Hello," Brea said. She hugged her bag of school supplies tightly against her chest.

"These are my friends," Roy said. "Brea, meet Jennet, Tam, and Marny."

"We've met," Jennet said. "Good to see you again."

Brea gave an awkward nod, unsure of how to respond.

"Hi," Tam said, brushing his brown hair out of his eyes.

"So, you're the Irish girl," Marny said. "Where you from, exactly? A city? Someplace smaller?"

The question caught Brea by surprise and she bit her lip, desperately formulating an answer.

"The country, to be sure," she said. "In the west."

Her heart beat frantically. Why had she not invented a town, a family? Oh, how little she knew of mortal dealings. Their customs and expectations closed around her like a trap.

As if sensing her panic, Roy stepped forward. "Chill, Marns. No need to interrogate the girl."

"Just wondering," Marny said, her voice bland.

"Mmhm." Jennet gave Brea another considering look. The sunlight fell on her hair, gilding it with light. "We'd love to hear about where you're from."

"Maybe over food," Roy said. "I thought we could head to Zeg's simcafé."

"I could use a monster cookie," Tam said.

"Shotgun," Marny called, then shrugged at the look Roy gave her. "What? Brea will fit in back of your tiny car better than I can."

Brea glanced from one to the other, trying in vain to understand their conversation. Humans were beyond confusing.

"Or I could message my chauffeur," Jennet said. "He'd be happy to drive us."

"Nah, we'll squeeze," Tam said. "Let George have his afternoon off. You can sit on my lap."

He gave Jennet a smile so full of sweetness it sent a ripple of power through the air. Brea nearly gasped aloud at the effect. She knew, as all fey folk did, that human dreams and yearnings carried essential sustenance into the Realm of Faerie. Without mortal connection, the realm would wither and die—which was why the queen had impelled her forth on her quest.

But never before had Brea been close enough to mortals to experience the impact of such pure emotion. Her body hummed, and she felt her wellspring of magic replenish.

Perhaps it was not so terrible, to be forced into dealing with these particular humans.

"Come on." Roy turned and led them toward a flat gray expanse of concrete that held a number of vehicles.

He stopped in front of a bright red car and unlocked the doors with a flourish.

"It's a little cramped," he said, opening the door and folding the seat forward so that she could clamber inside. "Sorry."

She could not muster a reply—all her attention was focused on not touching the frame of the vehicle. Though it was cased in a plastic material, the metal bones of the car buzzed like a nest of wasps, warning her to approach no closer. Cold iron was inimical to the fey folk—and she was no exception.

Yet she could not suddenly decline to go with them, despite the sickness she felt rising in her belly. Taking a deep breath, Brea ducked her head and stepped into the heart of the enemy.

CHAPTER NINE

Bʀᴇᴀ sʟɪᴘᴘᴇᴅ into the back of Roy's grav-car, careful not to touch the frame. The buzz of cold iron set her teeth on edge as she perched on the seat, holding her arms and legs tightly against her body. The extra magic she'd absorbed from Tam and Jennet's affection helped buffer her, and she was intensely grateful for it. Next time, she would meet Roy and his friends at their chosen destination, instead of traveling with them in the intense discomfort of a metal vehicle.

If there was a next time.

Tam plopped down on the seat next to her, and Jennet slid onto his lap. He put his arms around her, and she smiled and leaned back against him. The wash of human emotion spilling from them helped mute the hard hum of the car's iron.

"Buckle up back there," Marny called from the front seat. "You know how Roy drives."

"Like a god," Roy said, his voice tinged with irony.

"Of the underworld," Marny shot back. "Let's just get to my uncle's café in one piece."

Jennet pulled a strap from the side of the seat and fastened it around her and Tam. Watching from the corner of her eye, Brea tried to emulate her. She found the strap, where a metal buckle dangled. Her hand brushed against it, and she jerked her fingers away, her skin stinging.

"Here." Jennet grabbed the buckle and snicked it into place. "Roy's seatbelts are finicky."

It seemed a reasonable explanation, but there was something knowing in her blue eyes that made Brea's fear rise again. Could Jennet suspect what she was?

No. This was the modern mortal world. They no longer understood the ways of Faerie. The old roads were closed, the sacred clearings razed, the standing stones long since toppled to make way for human habitation.

"I am unused to this type of car," she said to Jennet.

"Roy has the newest, fanciest toys," Tam said. "Very few people can afford to ride around in this particular brand sports car."

"Do they have grav-cars where you're from?" Jennet asked.

Brea almost said *no*, then caught herself. Oh, this mortal girl was clever.

"There are grav-cars in Ireland, of course," she said, hoping it was so. "But not many in my area of habitation."

At least that part was the truth.

Roy made a quick turn, and she was forced to brace herself for a moment against the side of the car. The hidden metal beneath her touch vibrated, sending a surge of dizziness through her.

After what felt like an eternity, the car came to halt. Jennet pushed the buttons to release both of their seatbelts, and Brea gave her a grateful glance. Roy hopped out and folded his seat forward, then extended his hand to help her disembark. It was a curiously courtly gesture.

Brea took his hand. The touch of his fingers steadied her, and helped to banish the chill lingering against her skin. As soon as she was free of the car, she made herself let go. It would not do to become too accustomed to human touch. No matter how good it might feel.

"Here we are," Marny said. "Best simcafé in town."

They stood before a store fronted with brightly lit windows. Through the glass, Brea could see a long counter with stools ranged along its length. The walls were bright with posters, and one side of the café held a collection of gaming machines.

Roy followed her gaze. "Do you sim?"

"Ah." She blinked, trying to recall what she had seen of simming on the vids. "No, I am not experienced with sim systems."

"How about screens?" Marny asked. "That's my mode, though the rest of the gang are some fierce simmers."

"One day, Marny," Roy said.

The big girl shook her head. "Nope." She turned her attention to Brea, the question still lighting her face.

"I am not much by way of playing machine games," Brea said. "Where I come from... you might call it backwards, I suppose. There is little technology."

"Then we'll have to teach you," Roy said, giving her a wide smile.

Brea was not so sure. Even if the gaming machines were

made from plas-metal, she was so unfamiliar with human interfaces she would certainly fail spectacularly.

Which might not be a bad thing, for then Roy and his friends would see she had no skill and cease pressing her. Indeed, perhaps she should aim to be unsuccessful. The thought gave her a twinge she did not want to examine more closely. What should she care how these humans saw her? Her worth in their eyes was meaningless.

Tam held the door open, and the five of them entered the café. The bright lights overhead reflected off the gaming machines and a small scattering of tables. Large potted plants stood between the windows, and the air smelled of coffee and plastic mixed together. Random noises emitted from the machines: beeps and dings and a snatch of music played over and over. An open doorway into the back room showed a glimpse of elaborate sim systems in a rainbow of colors.

A man who much resembled a bear in both size and furriness looked up from his place behind the counter. His teeth gleamed, framed by his large beard, as he grinned at them.

"Hey, team!" He rose and came out to greet them.

"Uncle Zeg." Marny gave him a big hug.

Jennet hugged him, too, while Roy and Tam exchanged with him the obligatory handshake/backslap human males seemed to favor. Brea hung back, shyness stealing her voice.

"Who's this?" Zeg asked, tipping his head toward her. "Another gamer you guys have discovered, hiding out in Crestview?"

"She's new," Marny said. "Exchange student from Ireland, and not much of a gamer."

"Yet," Roy said.

"I am Brea Cairgead," she said, giving Zeg a slight bow.

She did not feel comfortable putting herself forward into his shadow, though he seemed kind enough. Still, his large and grizzled countenance roused old memories of hunter and prey.

"I see," Zeg said. "Well, Miss Brea, care for a cup of tea?"

"Certainly." Though no mortal food could pass her lips, she found she enjoyed tasting the various liquids.

The water of Crestview was tainted with chemicals, so she had discovered bottled water, as well as sweetened juices and teas. Carbonated beverages made her sneeze, however, and she'd no interest in sampling the coarse alcohols concocted by humans.

"Everyone else, your usual?" Zeg asked.

They nodded, confirming Brea's impression that Roy and his friends spent a great deal of time at the café.

She trailed them up to the counter. Jennet and Tam perched on stools at one end, Marny scooting in next to them. Roy took the next stool, then patted the one beside him in invitation. She sat, feeling very much pulled along by the current. So she would try to swim where it took her, and leap free if necessary. For now, though, what better way for her to brush a bit of magic against these mortals? She could slowly build up their vulnerability to the realm, rather than trying to convey it all in a single blast.

In particular, Roy seemed an excellent target. She had studied the ways of courtship among humans, and knew she could not approach Tam with "accidental" touches. Marny would make another good prospect, though she held herself at a distance.

No, for now Brea would focus on Roy. To that end, she summoned her magic. It seeped through her, thin as moonlight, a pale, quiet power. Carefully, she set her fingers to the back of his hand, where it rested on the counter. She meant it to be a casual gesture, but the feel of his bare skin shocked through her, even as she sent a silver flare of magic forth.

He jerked his head up, his eyes meeting hers. The words, the breath, died in her throat. She felt as though she could fall into the still pools of his eyes, submerge herself in those depths and lose herself. Her heart beat loud within her chest as she held his gaze.

"Here you are," Zeg said, setting a mug of tea before her.

Awareness returned in a rush—the sharp scent of fresh-brewed herbs, the bright lights, the beeping and chirping of the game machines against the wall.

Roy raised one eyebrow, and heat swept into her cheeks. Hastily, she drew her hand back. Triumph and confusion swirled through her in a disquieting mix. She was affecting him, there was no question. But she was unprepared for the influence he had over her own senses, a giddy, breathless feel like the sparkle of sunlight on a clear lake.

"I am glad you brought me here," she said, then busied herself with her tea, avoiding the questions she sensed in his eyes.

"You're welcome," he said, a note of puzzlement in his voice.

She turned the cup back and forth on the countertop. Roy's presence beside her felt like the pull of the sun, and she a wayward star who had strayed too close. A quick sip of tea steadied her, the warm, minty taste soothing on her tongue.

She drew in a breath and reminded herself to blend in, to appear as normal as she could.

"Which games are your favorite?" she asked.

"Oh, just about anything. Though nothing can compare to sim immersion. You've really never simmed before?"

She shook her head, aware that Marny watched her curiously.

"Can't blame her," the dark-haired girl said. "Simming isn't for everyone."

"She has to at least try before she can dismiss it," Roy said. "Most people like that feeling of being transported into the game. Of fully being there, in the environment. Experiencing it."

"I think you should start with a screenie or old-school vid game," Marny said, taking a bite of the large cookie Zeg had set before her.

"And so we will." Roy swiveled on his stool to face the wall of game systems. "Any of those look good to you, Brea?"

She turned and pondered the row of machines. The lights and sounds bewildered her senses. On one screen, cartoonish grav-cars raced, blurring through a landscape full of colorful trees until one spun out of control up onto the blue grasses. On another machine, a pair of stylized fighters circled one another, trading blows with glowing swords and leaping acrobatically back and forth.

A third screen depicted a boy with a pole dangling into the water. The line jerked, and he pulled it up, exclaiming at the huge fish he'd hooked. She swallowed and turned her attention to the last machine in the row.

"What is that one?" she asked, gesturing to the slanted, boxlike interface.

An array of colorful buttons adorned the front, and the top resembled a maze, with flashing lights and spinning balls of color.

"Virtual Pinball," Roy said. "Want to give it a try?"

She took a sip of her hot, sweet tea, and continued to eye the machine. Of all the games, it appeared to be the most approachable.

"Here." Zeg laid a magnetized card on the counter, bearing the logo of his café. "Play's on the house this afternoon."

She blinked up at him, trying to understand.

"Thanks," Roy said, picking up the card. "I'd be happy to treat you, too, Brea. Maybe next time."

Ah—one needed a form of currency to be able to pay for the games. She glanced at Roy's wrist, where an embedded chip gleamed. While she understood the concept of money, she'd had no use for it so far. But most humans paid for their needs using an elaborate system of scanning and debits that she had no hope of unraveling.

Thus far, her innate fey abilities and small magics had given her access to everything she needed. This was a new complication, one she would need to give further thought to.

"My appreciation," she said, nodding to Zeg.

"You're welcome," he said, gravely.

She was glad he had not bared his teeth at her in his discomfiting grin.

"I'll play first," Marny said. "Show you the basics. Roy's no good at explaining anything game-related."

"Hey," Roy said, but there was a smile in his voice.

Marny slipped off her stool and went to the machine. Watching her move, Brea could see the family resemblance to her uncle. They were both big-boned and darker-skinned, though Marny, thankfully, did not remind her of a bear. She held out her hand, and Roy put the card in her palm. For a moment, wistful loneliness stirred in Brea's blood. She missed that wordless communication of kind to kind.

Well, she must be lonely a while more. There was nothing remotely like her in the mortal world. Except Puck, perhaps, but in truth he was unique among the fey folk.

"Okay," Marny said, swiping the card through the payment slot of the pinball game. "The goal is to rack up points and keep your ball in play as long as possible. You want to stay out of the drain at the bottom, or you lose your ball. Gather round."

The machine lit up and began playing a fast-paced tune with a thumping beat. Marny leaned forward and hit the bright yellow button. A glowing ball shot up the side of the machine to the top of the angled screen. The game itself was filled with garish artwork of lizard-like monsters and tropical flowers.

Brea leaned forward, watching from her vantage point along the side. Roy stood next to her, close enough that their arms brushed. She welcomed the tingle of his touch, but her attention remained fixed on the machine, on trying to understand the frenzied movements of the ball.

Marny flicked the animated levers at the bottom and sides of the game, clattering the little ball in and out of the mazelike portions. She nudged the side of the machine with her hip, and a row of bright flowers lit up, dinging.

"Bonus for hitting all four bumpers," Roy murmured. "If she can keep the ball in play in the garden area, she'll gain more points."

Brea glanced to the head of the machine, where Marny's score was illuminated in glowing yellow numbers, quickly increasing.

"She's going for the combo now." Roy pointed to a series of steps above a bright green lizard with huge fangs. "She's got to go around the hibiscus loop, bouncing off each step at a time. If she makes it, she'll get a multiball. But if she loses control, the lizard will eat her ball and that round will be over. It's a tricky move to pull off."

The ball bounced wildly, going at a speed Brea could not imagine being able to direct. Marny's focus was intent, her hands constant on the levers. She paused, then hit, then paused again. The machine clattered and buzzed. One step, then two. The last one seemed most perilous. Brea leaned forward.

The ball missed, the green lizard opened its mouth, and Roy shook his head as the machine played a descending fanfare.

"Almost," Tam said. "That was an ambitious move."

"Sometimes you have to take risks." Marny didn't seem unduly upset by her loss. "There's still a couple more balls left to play. Brea, are you ready?"

She was not, but there was no sense in waiting. The blurring colors and ricocheting ball would not suddenly become familiar in the space of an afternoon, no matter how many games she watched. And there was no substitute for experience, nerve-racking though it might be.

"Certainly." She took Marny's place at the end of the machine, then eyed the controls. Thank the moon and stars the entire table was made of plastic, and the interface, while simulating metal bits, was nothing more than light and pixels.

"Pull and release the spring to send the ball in," Marny said, indicating the lower right corner. A new silver ball sat waiting atop the graphic of a wound spring.

Heart pounding, Brea set her fingers to the spring icon and drew it back. The ball shot into the heart of the game.

"Use the flippers," Roy said, coming to stand at her shoulder. "The bottom ones control the uppers, too."

She flicked them forward, and one hit the ball with a satisfying thwack. Back up it went, bumping about in the flowery area. The colorful blossoms lit up and dinged.

"Nice one," Jennet said. "Keep it going."

Brea tried, but her flipper missed and the ball plummeted down, away from anywhere she could reach. It fell into a pocket and stopped.

"Now what?" She glanced up at Roy, distracted by the warmth in his eyes.

"You're in the kickout. The ball will get back into play —now. Go."

She turned her attention back to the machine, crashing the flippers up and down. One good strike, another, and then the ball careened to one side, slid down the lane, and was gone.

"Oh." She was surprised at her sense of disappointment. "May I play again?"

"Sure," Marny said. "And try unfocusing your eyes a little. It helps."

Brea sent the next ball spinning up into the machine. This

time she ignored Roy standing beside her, let her gaze soften, and leaned forward.

Flip. Bounce and ricochet. Blink and spin and whirl. Around and around the silvery ball went, and slowly she began to feel the predictable grace and gravity of it. Use the levers hard and fast—then back off and wait. There was a trick to the upper flippers, to keeping the ball dancing. The flowers lit up, one by one. The lizard monsters roared, but went hungry.

Suddenly another ball joined the first, this one bigger and golden-hued. Moon and sun, ebb and flow. She welcomed its orbit into the blinking lights of her own small universe, let it whirl and soar.

Dimly, she was aware of a bell pinging.

"No way," Tam said. "She's going to crush your high score, Marny."

"Guess I'm a good teacher."

Brea paid their conversation little heed. There was nothing but the quick race of the balls within the machine. Once, she almost lost them, but recalled Marny's hip bump. The game blinked, then kept going as the balls spun back into the center of play.

At last, the golden ball fell away. As if missing its companion, the silver one soon followed. The frenzy of lights and colors faded. Dazed, Brea looked up.

"Wow." Roy laid his hand on her back. "That was amazing."

She leaned into his touch, feeling suddenly drained. Had she unconsciously been using magic while she played?

"Enter your name," Jennet said.

Brea blinked at her, uncomprehending.

"You've set the new high score on the game." The blonde girl smiled. "Here, use the keypad."

The backboard of the machine was alight with a monstrously high number, followed by a blinking underscore. Slowly, Brea typed the letters of her human first name. How long would it stay inscribed there, at the top of a mortal pinball game? Only hours, or perhaps years. It was a curious thought, that her high score might remain long after she had left the human world.

"Prime playing," Tam said. "You should seriously enter some tournaments."

"I do not think so." Brea grasped for the term, found it. "It was beginner's luck. I would like to see the rest of you play."

Roy grinned. "I don't know if any of us can top your score."

"Maybe not today," Marny said, cocking up one eyebrow. "But Tam can't resist a challenge."

"Me?" Tam gave her a look of false astonishment. "Speak for yourself."

"Hey, gang, don't forget your tea and cookies," Zeg called from the counter.

"Yes, Mom," Marny said, and they all laughed good-naturedly and returned to their abandoned snacks.

Gratefully, Brea downed the rest of her tea. She listened quietly as the others joked about gaming, relaxing into the warmth of their camaraderie. For a short while, she could pretend she truly was what she appeared to be: a human girl, finding new friends in a foreign land.

CHAPTER TEN

Roy watched Brea slowly return from the post-game haze of playing pinball. He knew the disorientation of immersing back into the real world, all too well. All gamers did.

Trying to act like it was nothing, he went around behind her to give her a quick shoulder rub. She sighed a little and leaned into his hands.

"This okay?" he asked.

"Yes." Her voice held the touch of a smile, and he wished he could see her face.

"I always get tight when I game," he said. "Especially on a new machine. Take a deep breath in."

She did, and he pressed his thumbs in, then let up.

"Ah." She exhaled a contented sigh.

Jennet shot them a look, and he dropped his hands. Okay, he was being too transparent, but he couldn't help it. He hopped back on his own stool and tried to get Marny telling jokes. She seldom did, but once she got going, she was riotously funny.

Tam added a few lame knock-knock jokes that were so bad everyone laughed anyway. Even Brea.

The sound lit Roy up inside, maybe because it was so unexpected—light and lively, in contrast with her quiet demeanor. He really could not figure the girl out, but her mystery made her all the more interesting.

"It's getting late," Jennet said, glancing out the windows.

"Yep." Tam pushed back from the counter. "Marny, you staying here with Zeg, or walking with me?"

"I have homework," Marny said. "We'd better head."

"I can take you guys," Roy said.

"It's the opposite way from The View," Marny said. "We've had this argument before. Besides, I like the walk. Keeps me alert."

"Not nearly as alert as I had to be before we moved," Tam said.

"Then don't let me stop you two from practicing your ninja stealth skills." Roy turned to Brea. "We should get you home. Don't want your host family to worry."

The mirth in her face faded, like twilight seeping out of the sky as night fell.

"Do not concern yourself for me," she said. "I can escort myself home."

"It's no problem. Really." He glanced at Jennet. "We can take a detour on the way back to The View, right?"

"Sure," she said.

Brea shook her head, a small, anxious move. "There is no need."

"I think there is," he said.

Something was off, and her reluctance made him even

more determined to figure out what. Why wouldn't she tell them anything about her host family?

Tam stepped forward. "Don't push," he murmured. "Everyone's entitled to their secrets. Give it time."

Time. Right. Roy blew out an impatient breath. "How will you get home, Brea?"

"It is not so far from here," she said. "I will walk partway with Tam and Marny."

He glanced out the window. "It's getting dark, and we're a little too near the Exe for me to feel comfortable about that. No offense to your old stomping grounds, Tam."

"Then we should make haste, while there is still light in the sky." The corner of Brea's lips twitched, as though she were holding in a smile.

Though what she had to smile about, Roy had no idea.

"Do not fret for me, Royal," she said. "I will allow your friends to see me to my door."

"Sounds like a plan," Marny said. "Can we quit arguing about this already? I'm getting hungry."

"You're sure?" Roy put his hand on Brea's arm.

She covered it with her fingers, and again that curious warmth went through him. This girl affected him in the craziest way.

"I will see you tomorrow," she said. Her gaze held his, and he couldn't argue with her any more.

Marny tapped her foot while Tam and Jennet hugged, then kissed.

"Okay, okay. Enough with the love fest," Marny said. "Time to move out."

Brea stepped away from him, and Roy forced himself not

to follow like a lovesick puppy. They all gathered their bags and belongings and trooped to the door.

"Good night, team!" Zeg waved from behind the counter. "Stay out of trouble."

"We will if you will," Marny said to her uncle.

"Bye." Jennet waved, and Brea lifted her hand in farewell.

"Unlikely," Tam said. "See you next time, Zeg."

"You know it," Roy said.

He still wanted to get Brea on a sim system. She'd had such strong natural talent with the pinball, he was burning to see what she would do in a full immersion game.

On the sidewalk, they parted into two groups. Before Roy headed with Jennet to his car, he turned to Brea again.

"Walk safely," he said.

"I shall." Her voice was clear and confident.

Still, he didn't fire up his grav-car until she, Tam, and Marny had turned the corner.

"We can leave any time, Roy," Jennet said from the passenger seat. "Or are you planning to follow them all the way to Marny's?"

"No."

Although the thought had crossed his mind. He pulled a U-turn and headed up the street. The grav-car slid smoothly over the pitted road.

"Brea's safe with Tam, you know that."

"Yeah, but what is going on with Brea?"

"Other than the fact you're falling hard and fast for her?" Jennet asked.

"I'm not." He took the corner a little too quickly, making Jennet grab the door handle.

"Come on. You can't fool your friends."

"Until I know more about her, I'm not falling anywhere," he said. Strong words, but part of him knew it was already too late. "There's something tweaked about that girl, or her situation."

Jennet was silent a moment. Roy glanced over to see her chewing her lip in thought.

"Don't tell me you don't see it?" he asked.

"I do. And I'm glad you do, too. I can't help thinking it has something to do with Feyland."

"I don't think she was lying about her gaming experience," he said. "Or lack thereof. So if she's never simmed, how could Feyland be involved?"

He wanted to talk to Brea, really talk, somewhere quiet with just the two of them. Not that he was convinced she would confide in him, but there was something vulnerable in her expression, an echo of loneliness he understood.

Besides, he needed to make more sketches of her. She had a quality of stillness he ached to capture. If she'd let him.

"Maybe she's a faerie," Jennet said.

"What?" His stomach clenched in denial. "How could that even be possible? The Dark Queen can't transport creatures here at will. And if she could, I highly doubt she'd send one to impersonate a teenage girl. The Black Knight would be more likely." He accelerated, the streetlights flickering past.

"I know," Jennet said. "It's farfetched. But Puck can come through."

"Puck's outside the normal rules."

"And Aran said goblins came to get him."

"Yeah but they popped him in a sack and took him right

back to the realm. They didn't hang around pretending to be high school students. Seriously, Brea's not a faerie. Although... maybe something happened to her in Ireland. She stumbled into an enchanted stone circle or something."

"Maybe." Jennet sounded doubtful. "I thought Thomas explained that Feyland worked as a gateway to the realm because the places in our world were all gone. We need to get her in-game, see what happens."

"Okay." He suspected they wouldn't necessarily get any answers. "And I'll try and talk to her—one on one. If we all start pounding the question, we'll scare her off."

The car whooshed under the plas-metal arch of The View. Carefully groomed landscapes and lawns attached to spacious houses flashed past on either side. Some of them showed warm light in the windows, but about half were dark and empty. VirtuMax Corporation was still transferring its full staff to the new headquarters at Crestview—whether they wanted to come or not.

"Invite Brea over this weekend," Jennet said. "Good thing you have four FullD systems."

"Yeah."

Jennet glanced over at him. "Pay attention, Roy. Don't let your attraction to her make you oblivious."

"Oh, I'm paying attention. Whatever's going on with that girl, we'll figure it out."

As the red grav-car turned the corner, Brea let out a quiet breath of relief. She would not have to endure riding inside that metal body, nor be subject to Jennet's keen-eyed glances.

Certainly, she must still mislead Tam and Marny, but it would be easier to do in the open air.

"Where to?" Tam asked.

She lifted her head, sensing the sure direction of where her bolt-hole lay. Not that she would lead them anywhere near her refuge, but it was a start.

"That way," she said, pointing down the street.

"Good," Marny said. "We're headed that direction, too."

She strode down the sidewalk, and Tam and Brea followed.

"You and Marny share a dwelling?" Brea asked him.

The notion confused her. Although they were friends, there did not seem to be any familial or romantic ties between them.

"No." Tam stuck his hands in his pockets. "My mom and brother and I live in an apartment on the same block."

The tightness in his voice cautioned her not to pry, and so she did not. Dusk thickened about them as they walked, the last bit of light smearing the western sky. Orange-tinged streetlights flicked on. All the stores they passed were closed, their windows shuttered or darkened, or in some instances, boarded over.

"What street are you on?" Tam asked after some silent minutes of walking.

"Ah." She had never paid much heed to the bent and rusted street signs in the Exe. "I am not certain of the name—but we will need to go left at the next turning."

Obviously she could not create her illusion here, in the midst of a commercial block. Her nerves fluttered. Could she truly deceive these mortals in such a way?

Nonsense. She was fey, and capable of things beyond human ken. To her relief, the shops quickly gave way to houses. Surely what she needed lay ahead…

Her soft leather boots did not have laces to become untied, so she must make do with a different subterfuge.

"One moment," she said. "I have a stone in my shoe."

"Marny," Tam called. "Wait up."

Under cover of removing her boot, Brea sent her faerie-sight forward, past where Marny had halted, hands on her hips. Past the street crossing, around a corner… oh, there must be the type of place she sought, somewhere!

There. To the stop sign, and then two blocks to the right. She swayed with relief, and Tam caught her elbow, bringing her abruptly back into her body.

"You okay?"

"Yes." Now that she had found her answer.

She slipped her boot back on, and they hurried to catch up with Marny. At the street corner, Brea took the lead.

"We are almost there," she said, taking the right-hand turning.

"Who's your host family, again?" Marny asked, her dark eyes narrowed with suspicion.

"Mr. and Mrs. Lee." It was the name of a family on one of the vids she had been watching.

"Do they have kids?" Tam asked.

"Their son, Sam, is younger than I am."

"I don't know any Sam Lee at Crestview," Marny said.

"Oh, he is too young to attend Crestview High," Brea said, keeping her tone light. "There's the house, that blue one in the middle."

It was not easy, conversing while trying to throw an illusion. Still, her store of magic was replenished enough. And spinning illusions was simpler than attempting to influence human minds, or imbuing them with vulnerability to fey magic.

"Is anyone home?" Tam asked.

Brea concentrated, and a light in the upstairs window went on. "They are usually in the back," she lied. "Watching vids."

She stumbled as she stepped off the sidewalk, but nimbly regained her footing. Although she had caused a trim lawn and walkway to appear, the true nature of the uneven ground was evident beneath her feet.

"We'll walk you to the door," Tam said.

"No!" She swallowed. "I mean, that is not necessary. I have a key."

Marny tilted her head, her gaze going to the upper window.

"Everything okay with you in there?" she asked. "Because if you're in any trouble, we can help."

The words, unexpected and sincere, warmed Brea. For a brief moment, the taste of her deception was sour on her tongue. But these were humans, not her allies.

"That is most kind," she said. "But all is well, I assure you. Good night."

Without giving either of them time to accompany her, she darted up to the porch—which was in truth the edge of a long-abandoned crumbling foundation. Pretending to dig in her pockets, she produced an illusory silver key, and made a show of unlocking the door. She opened it, feigned turning on the lights, then waved at Tam and Marny where they still stood on the sidewalk, facing the house.

Tam lifted one hand in farewell, but Marny just watched, her expression set.

Brea closed the false door, her hands trembling. She could not maintain the illusion for much longer. *Go*, she thought. *I am safe.*

After a moment, Tam shrugged and said something to Marny. She nodded, and the two of them continued down the street. Brea watched them through the transparency of her illusory house. At last, they turned the corner and were gone.

Brea held her illusion a heartbeat longer, then let it unravel, keeping only a corner of the shadows to wrap herself in. Cloaked in night, she slipped over the broken ground and set her steps toward her true refuge, nestled deep within the decay of the Exe.

CHAPTER ELEVEN

Roy dropped Jennet off at her house, then headed home. Dinner would be ready soon, and despite eating one of Zeg's monster cookies, he was hungry.

"*Master Lassiter,*" the house said as he stepped in from the garage. "*Your presence is required in the study.*"

Damn. The hunger in his belly turned to a cold knot. The study was his mother's domain—which meant she was home, and she wanted to talk to him about something serious.

"I'll be right there," he said.

Every time she got a communication from his father, she called Roy in to play him the vid or read him the message. Then she'd rant for at least half an hour about how unreliable artists were, how she'd worked herself to the bone to make VirtuMax the premier corporation it was, and for what? So that her feckless husband could jaunt all over the globe, taking pictures of vanishing animals and places, and sell them for a pittance, shedding responsibility and neglecting his family.

The study door swung open at Roy's approach, light

sliding across the polished wood panels. He braced himself for his mother's acid words. Though seldom directed at him, they still left pits and scars. He didn't really blame his dad for not being around much, though he missed the guy. But more like you'd miss an older brother who'd gone off to college than a dad.

"Royal." His mother stood behind her gleaming steel desk, still wearing her work clothes—a dark blue suit, with no touches of color. "Come in. I have something to discuss with you."

On the shiny expanse of the desk, his non-school tablet sat, the screen glowing. His throat closed, and he forced himself to swallow past the tightness. Whatever this was about, it wasn't his dad.

"What's up?"

He knew, though, and went even colder inside.

"This." She pointed to his tablet, her brown eyes hard.

"You have no right to—"

"I have every right. I'm your mother, and you are my responsibility. Now, explain."

She picked up the tablet, her movements brisk with anger, and swiped through the images. An abstract swirl of blues and oranges, where he'd been playing with complementary colors. A leaf, rendered in painstaking detail. A series of half-drawn impressions of buildings. A clumsy illustration of a bird.

Brea, sketched in profile.

"She's a new girl at school," he said, part of him trying to pretend it was a small issue, that his mom was pissed that he had a portrait of a girl in his sketchbook—when he knew the real problem was that he had a sketchbook at all.

"I don't care. Your grades—never spectacular to begin with —are falling, you refused the internship I arranged at Virtu-Max, your friends are questionable at best—"

"My friends are some of the best people around."

His mother ignored the comment. "Not only is doodling a waste of your time, it's insulting to me, and to your future."

"I don't want to be a data cruncher or programmer, Mom."

"You have a legacy to inherit. VirtuMax will be—"

"I don't care. VirtuMax is *your* company, not mine. I have other plans for my life. I don't want yours. I don't want VirtuMax."

There, he'd said the words at last, in a way she could finally hear.

His mother stared at him, her lips set in a thin red line. She glanced down at his tablet and her nostrils flared. Then slowly, deliberately, she hit the delete button. Brea's sketch went black.

"Hey! Stop it." He lunged forward, reaching for his tablet.

His mother stepped back, quickly paging through his artwork and deleting every piece. Sprawled partway across the desk, Roy glared at her, his anger hardening into something solid and impermeable.

When she had finished, she handed his tablet back to him. His empty, useless tablet.

"I don't expect to see you attempt any more juvenile art. Not if you want your college paid for. Do you understand?"

"Oh yeah. I get it."

"And don't expect to restore your files. I found and wiped your chipdrive, as well." She sounded so coldly superior.

Roy held his tablet loosely in one hand, but his jaw was

clenched in rage, and in the certain knowledge his mother would cut him off if he crossed her in this.

"Also, your grav-car has been disabled for two weeks. You might want to inquire if the Carters' driver can take you to school during the interim."

"Fine." He grated the word out. "I won't be down for dinner."

It was a petty rebellion, but it was all he could manage for the moment. He whirled and stalked to the door.

She waved her hand in dismissal. "I was expecting as much. The staff will bring you up a tray. Good night."

Bitterness flared through him. For way too long, he'd let his mother control every aspect of his life. He'd even enjoyed it, most of the time. Being the prince of VirtuMax had its definite perks.

But now, it was a rope around his neck.

He'd find some way to slip free, though. He had to, if he wanted to keep breathing.

The past few months had shown him there was more out there than the narrow, if luxurious, walls he'd been raised inside. Real people, real friends, real emotions that, even if they burned, at least *meant* something.

CHAPTER TWELVE

THE DIN of Crestview High's halls barely penetrated Roy's mood. With only five weeks left until the end of the school year, people were getting boisterous, but he couldn't even manage a smile. He stalked toward his Literature classroom, paying little attention to the students around him.

"You're looking grim," Marny said, moving up to walk alongside him. "What's going on?"

Trust Marny to cut to the truth. Sometimes her straightforward manner bothered him, but today, not so much.

Maybe it would be good to talk to somebody about what was going on. The anger and disappointment bubbling inside him had to spill over, or he felt like he'd explode. And with Marny, he wouldn't have to spend a lot of time explaining. She was damn quick, and would be able to follow along.

"My mom..." He hesitated, then kept going in a rush. "She found my art files, and deleted them all."

Marny gave him a quick glance. She didn't laugh, or even act surprised at the fact that he was making art. Another good thing about her—she mostly accepted things without judging. Much.

"What are you going to do?" she asked.

He hunched his shoulders in response. "Not draw at home, clearly. Or keep anything on my tablets."

"Are you only working in digital mediums?"

"Pretty much." The few pencil and paper sketches he'd tried were laughably bad.

"Maybe you should branch out. The community center offers oil painting classes over the summer. And doesn't Jennet have a million empty rooms in her house?"

It was an intriguing suggestion—but right now he couldn't think past the black cloud in his head.

"Maybe. Here's my class."

"Right," she said. "See you at lunch."

He lifted his hand in farewell. Marny gave him one of her half-smiles, like she already knew he was thinking about what she'd said. She was too smart for Crestview—the school *and* the town.

One more year and she was so going to leave the dust of it behind.

So would he, of course, but probably not quite with the certainty or confidence of Marny.

Roy took his usual seat in the boring beige classroom and pulled out his tablet. Without thinking, he opened his drawing program and started doodling, like he always did between classes.

Dammit.

Impatiently, he brushed his hand over the screen, erasing the lines he'd just drawn. Sure, he could make some pictures, but he'd have to wipe them when he was done. Or dump them onto his chipdrive—but the whole thing felt useless. Even then, his mom might find that and destroy the data again.

Marny was right. He needed an offsite place where he could keep a tablet dedicated to his artwork. And maybe even mess around with physical mediums.

"Class, open your documents to location 5483," the teacher called.

Roy pulled in a deep breath, feeling the weight on his chest lighten. Maybe he could make things work—with a little help from his friends.

At lunch, he spied Brea hesitating in the hallway by the cafeteria doors.

"Hey," he said, touching her lightly on the arm. "Join us?"

The contact sent a sizzle of static through him, and he pulled his hand back, fingers tingling.

"Have you been playing with the ion field in science class?" he asked. "That was quite a charge."

She looked up at him, her eyes startled. "My apologies."

"There's a panel in the lab wall, where you put your hands to discharge the static buildup. You don't want to go around shocking people."

"I will remember that, for next time," she said.

Roy regarded her a long moment. It couldn't be easy, coming into a new culture, a new school when the year was almost over.

"How long are you here for?" he asked.

"I…" She swallowed, then darted a look into the cafeteria. "Your friends are waiting."

"Come on. We better grab our trays, then."

She was so skittish, he was afraid of scaring her off completely. But once she relaxed, he was going to get some answers. And some sketches, since he'd have to start over with his art.

"Hey," he said. "Do you have a free period here at school?"

She gave him a confused look.

"A time when you don't have a class," he clarified, gesturing for her to precede him in the lunch line.

Not that the cafeteria food was anything to get excited about. He eyed the grayish beans and limp hot dogs, the buns that tasted like cardboard, and the too-pink wriggle of the gelatin dessert, and let out a sigh.

"Oh, yes," she said. "The fifth period."

"Want to meet me in the library?" He had Computing then, but it was a mind-numbing class, easy to skip.

"I…" She glanced at him, then back at the unappetizing food on her tray. "Yes, I would like that."

"Great." He had Art right after lunch, and could grab a sketchbook and pencils. Maybe leave them at school, where his mom wouldn't bother to look.

He took a bottle of water and set it on his tray, frowning at the food. In addition to grounding his car, his mom had also decreed he didn't merit the privilege of chef-packed lunches for the next two weeks. Today, he'd decided to take his chances with the school food, but now he regretted it. Really, Crestview High was kidding itself if it thought the cafeteria lunches were anywhere near edible.

Brea looked resigned as she carried her tray to the table where Jennet, Tam, and Marny waited.

"Is the food better where you're from?" he asked.

"Oh, yes." An actual smile lit her face for a moment.

Roy blinked at the way the expression changed her features, taking her from pretty to stunning. Then she ducked her head, as if embarrassed that he'd seen her smile.

Not looking at him, she slid into the space beside Marny.

Roy stood at the head of the table for a second. He usually sat next to Marny, with Jennet and Tam across. Would Brea feel more comfortable with him facing her, or beside her?

"Sit by the girl, already," Marny said. "She knows you're not going to bite."

"I don't need your input," Roy said, but he moved to put his tray beside Brea's.

Across the table, Jennet shot him a grin, but Tam seemed more serious. As soon as Roy was settled, Tam leaned forward.

"I think we need to head into Feyland again," he said.

Beside him, Brea's fork clattered to the floor.

"Sorry," she said, ducking to retrieve it. "The dessert is rather slippery."

"Always is." Marny took a bite of her hot dog and then grimaced.

She and Tam usually made a fair stab at finishing their lunches, no matter how nasty. They didn't live in houses full of abundant food, the way Roy and Jennet did. Sometimes, he suspected school lunch was the only meal of Tam's day. But the guy was way too stubborn and proud, and Roy knew any offers of assistance—or extra meals—would be rejected.

"Tam and I talked," Jennet said. "Don't you think it would be fun to take Brea in-game with us?"

She gave Roy a significant look. Obviously, they couldn't

discuss Brea with her sitting right there, but it was clear Jennet and Tam felt that something was off.

And he had to agree, though he still wasn't convinced it had anything to do with Brea.

Late last night, Roy had woken, hot and sheet-tangled, the echo of a fey hunting horn ringing in his ears. He'd lain there a long time, listening, but it wasn't repeated. Still, any hint that the Wild Hunt might be riding in the mortal world was severely bad news.

Even if it was only a scrap of magic escaped through the gateway, and not the hunt itself, he could feel trouble simmering on the horizon.

"All right, let's game," he said. "Since tomorrow's Saturday, how about then. Early afternoon?"

"Works for me," Tam said.

"Brea, please join us," Jennet said. "I think you could pick up simming fairly quickly."

Roy felt Brea stiffen beside him, but her expression gave no flicker of emotion.

"I am not certain I am accomplished enough to do so." She looked up at him, something elusive flashing in her eyes. Fear? Yearning?

"You'll do great," he said. "We can teach you all the simming tricks. Did you know that Tam could've gone to the big national tournament? He's that good."

He'd never gotten the full story about why Tam hadn't made it after winning the regionals, but Roy strongly suspected it had to do with finances. Or lack thereof.

"Don't pressure the girl." Marny frowned over at him. "If

she decides she doesn't want to play, or doesn't like the equip, that's her choice."

Roy lifted his chin. "I'm not that guy anymore."

The completely arrogant one, who had power and used it to get his way, no matter the consequences. The one who'd made some less-than-prime choices. He didn't blame Marny for giving him the evil eye.

"We know you've changed," Jennet said—always the peacemaker.

"So let me prove it." Roy took a swallow from his bottled water to ease the tightness in his throat.

Yes, they wanted to get Brea in-game and see if she reacted with Feyland in any unusual way, but not by force or coercion.

"You in?" he asked, touching her shoulder.

Warmth spread through him from that point of contact, and he let his hand stay there a moment longer, hoping she wouldn't pull away. The silky material of her shirt was soft under his fingertips.

"Very well," she said, after a long pause. "I will game with you tomorrow."

"Good," Tam said from across the table. "Roy, you get to play taxi."

"Um." He dropped his gaze to his uneaten lunch. "My grav-car's grounded for two weeks. Sorry."

"What happened?" Tam asked.

"Family stuff. I'll tell you later."

Much as he liked Brea, he wasn't going to reveal all his raw secrets in front of her. He didn't even know what Tam and Jennet would think. Roy Lassiter—artist. It was so outside the image he'd been projecting, he wasn't even close to comfortable with it.

Marny's expression turned sympathetic, but she didn't say anything.

"Brea and I can take the bus and walk up to The View," Tam said.

"Don't be silly." Jennet gave him a fond look. "I'll come with George to get you. I have to get Brea a visitor's pass, anyway."

Right. Roy had forgotten that most people couldn't just traipse up to The View and come through the gates. Well, if they had a wrist chip, they could, but ordinary townies, no. He'd noticed Brea didn't have a chip, but then put it out of his mind.

Made sense, though. She'd already told them there wasn't much tech where she came from, so of course she wouldn't have a wrist-chip implant.

"Pick me up first," Tam said. "Then we can swing by and get Brea. Say, around one?"

"I will be ready," Brea said, her tone giving the words deep importance.

"Don't worry." Jennet smiled at her from across the table. "Simming's not that scary."

Marny hmphed in disagreement, but before she could voice her dislike of sim equip once again, the bell blared. The clamor of people emptying their trays and calling to friends effectively ended the conversation.

Brea jumped up, her lunch barely touched. Come to think of it, Roy didn't think she'd taken a single bite—not that he blamed her.

"I'll get this." He rose and grabbed both their trays. "See you later."

She tilted her face up to his, and for a moment the din of the cafeteria fell away. Roy felt as if they were standing in some quiet, moonlit glade. His heart thumped, then steadied, as they stared at one another.

Then she blinked, her pale cheeks blushing with color, and dropped her gaze.

"Farewell," she said.

Leaving Roy holding the lunch trays, she joined the current of exiting students and was gone.

"Interesting girl," Marny said. It was neither praise nor condemnation. "Good luck there."

"Yeah." He felt his lips twist in a rueful smile. "I have a feeling I'm going to need it."

At fifth period, he hurried to the library, sketchbook and pencils tucked into his pack. Brea wasn't there yet, though a few students were scattered at the tables, studying. The screens were all occupied, but that didn't matter.

He headed toward the north windows and found an unoccupied table tucked partway into the corner. Then, to give himself something to do while he waited, he pulled out his art supplies and flipped to the first page. The pencils ranged from hard to soft. Some of them were not very sharp, and the gummy eraser was already dingy from use—but they'd do.

Three minutes until the bell. He hoped Brea would show, but didn't want to seem like he was just sitting there, anxiously awaiting her. Even though part of him felt that way.

Instead, he began to draw. A leaf, attached to a thorny

stem. A closed rosebud, shading from nearly black to pearl. His pencil slid, and he paused to grab the eraser.

"You are very talented." Brea's voice sounded from right beside him.

He looked up, startled. "I didn't see you there."

"I can be very quiet," she said, her eyes sparkling with secret amusement.

"Well, sit down." He started to close the sketchbook, but Brea held out her hand.

She studied his drawing a few moments more, then met his gaze.

"I believe you have the soul of an artist, Royal Lassiter," she said.

His heart knocked loudly in his chest. "Not that it's going to get me anywhere."

She rounded the table and sat, then reached over and lightly touched his hand. His pulse jumped again at the contact.

"If you have such a gift, you must share it with the world," she said. "Such skill should not be hidden away. Would you show me more of your art?"

"I don't have anything else. Not here."

"Oh." She looked genuinely disappointed. "Then you must make more."

The soft light from the window shone over her hair and made her fair skin glow.

"Actually, would you mind if I sketched you?"

"Me?" Her eyes widened. "Surely I am no fitting subject."

"Let me draw you, and you'll see how pretty you are."

A faint blush touched her cheeks. "Surely you flatter me."

"Only a little." He grinned at her, suddenly feeling that what she'd said might be true. Maybe he did have a future as an artist, after all. "Say yes."

"Very well." She sat up, her back stiff, and stared past his left shoulder, her face set. "I am ready."

"No, no. Relax back into the chair. There you go. Turn your head to the window just a little. Now... think about home."

Her expression softened into wistfulness, the line of her mouth smoothing, her eyes widening.

"Perfect," Roy said. "Stay that way for just a bit."

He drew quickly, trying to capture the basic lines of her cheeks and forehead and especially her nose. Not quite right. Flip the page, try again. Finally, he was satisfied.

"Are you finished?" she asked.

"Not at all, but you can move now if you want." His pencil swooshed across the page as he filled in the shading under her neck, added a bit of shadow to her hair.

She let out a quiet breath and leaned forward, resting her elbows on the table.

"Why are you named Royal?" she asked.

"Because my mom has delusions of grandeur," he said. "Getting a PhD and becoming top CEO of one of the biggest companies in the world is as close as she can get to being a queen."

Brea shivered and glanced away. "Why did she not name you Prince, instead?"

"That would be even worse. Or King."

"Ruler?" Her voice lightened. "Monarch of All?"

"Supreme Dictator of the Universe." Roy cracked up. "Yeah, okay, I guess my name isn't that bad."

"I like it. Royal."

"I like it when you say it, but only then. Here." He turned the sketch so she could view it. "What do you think?"

She stilled, and he held his breath, trying to read the depths in her eyes.

"I never knew I could be seen in such light," she said. "Thank you."

He smiled at her, relieved. "I'll make you a copy, if you like."

"I would—very much."

Somehow their hands met, their fingers weaving together. Roy wished there wasn't an expanse of table between them.

The bell blared, shattering the moment, and Brea jumped back.

"I shall see you tomorrow," she said, giving him the hint of a shy smile as she stood.

"You bet. And don't worry about playing Feyland. You'll do great."

She nodded once, then slipped away as silently as she'd come. Roy watched her go. Once she'd disappeared into the hallway, he looked down at his sketch. Satisfaction kindled through him.

"Yeah," he said quietly. "Not bad."

He'd make her a copy, but he felt as though Brea was the one who had given him a gift. It felt a lot like hope.

CHAPTER THIRTEEN

THE NEXT DAY, half an hour before the appointed time to go play Feyland, Brea went to the vacant lot and spun her illusion. Her interactions with Roy the day before had restored her powers, and it was a simple thing to create the façade of her nonexistent host family's house.

She sat on the sidewalk and let the late spring breezes play in her hair. The street was mostly deserted and quiet, except for one family leaving their house and driving away in a noisy vehicle that lacked the smooth grace of a grav-car. After that, stillness descended. To amuse herself, she called any stray blossoms in the vicinity.

A drift of white petals floated down the street; apple blossoms. They hovered about her like white moths for a moment, settling in her hair and decorating her gray sweater. It was woven of softest cashmere, and she found it much more comforting against her skin than the synthetic materials the humans favored. The cotton of her blue jeans was nearly as palatable, and sheep's wool socks cushioned her feet within her leather boots.

A sleek black grav-car turned the corner, and she rose, brushing petals from her shoulders. The sunshine and flowers had fortified her, but she still did not relish the notion of another journey trapped within a metal machine.

The car drew smoothly up to the curb beside her, and the door slid open.

"Hi," Jennet said, leaning partway out.

Brea did not miss the curious, lingering glance Jennet gave her "house," and hurriedly strengthened her illusion.

"Ready?" Tam asked from the seat beside Jennet.

Despite the discomfort shivering through her, Brea nodded. There was no other option. Following Jennet's gesture, she stepped into the surprisingly roomy vehicle. A second bench seat faced the one Tam and Jennet occupied. Brea sat, then breathed a grateful sigh when she discovered the cushion was covered with leather.

"Ready to go, back there?" a disembodied voice asked.

Startled, Brea looked around.

"That's George, the driver," Jennet said. "He's sitting on the other side of the panel. Which he really should leave down." Her voice rose in command.

A humming noise sounded beside Brea's ear, and the smoky pane of glass slid away, to reveal the front of the car. A man wearing a uniform and blue cap turned his head.

"If you wish, Miss Carter. Just thought you and Tam would like a little privacy on the way."

Jennet flushed, and Tam's hand tightened on her knee. The

air filled with brightness, and Brea eagerly absorbed it. Using the last bit of power, she coated her hands and quickly fastened the buckle of the seatbelt. The metal barely stung her fingers.

"We're good," Jennet said.

It took a moment for Brea to realize the vehicle was in motion. George drove skillfully, without any of the sudden turns or accelerations Roy seemed to favor. Riding facing backwards, combined with the toxic hum of metal around her, made her queasy. She swallowed, and concentrated on the subtle warmth still rippling out from Jennet and Tam.

After what felt an eternity, the ride ended. The door whooshed open, and she fumbled with her seatbelt, eager to be free. She ducked out of the vehicle and stood on the sidewalk, gratefully absorbing the fresh air. An ornate fountain played nearby, and the smell of earth and grass helped calm her racing heart, despite the taint of chemicals that overlay the lawn.

"Sorry about that," Jennet said, exiting the car. "I should have switched places with you. I forgot how sick-making riding backwards can be."

"I am much recovered," Brea said.

Tam led the way up the flagstone walk. As he passed the fountain, a spray of water flew toward him.

"Hey!" He jumped back.

"Roy's fountain is malfunctioning again." Jennet grinned. "I think it likes you."

Brea could not share in their mirth, for there, in the shallow basin, lay a sharp-toothed nixie. Invisible to the humans, of course, she gave Brea a penetrating glare—one water creature to another, staking out her territory.

How had another fey being come to inhabit such a place? It did not bode well.

"Coming?" Tam asked from the imposing granite entryway of the mansion.

Though it made her spine shiver to turn her back on the nixie, Brea hurried to where the mortals awaited. The huge double doors of the house swung open, and she followed Tam and Jennet inside. The high laughter of the nixie was mercifully cut off by the thud of the doors closing.

Brea's relief evaporated quickly as she glanced about the cavernous foyer. Sconces mounted on the walls provided dim light, and every surface was hard and polished, from the marble floors to the metallic-looking walls. It was chilly, too, and although coolness usually did not bother her, she did not like the emptiness of the air. There was no warmth of emotion. No love. Brea took a step closer to Tam and Jennet, letting the constant energy of their affection wash over her.

"*Your guests have arrived,*" an inhuman voice announced. The synthetic tones echoed down the hallway.

"I wish Roy would change his house's speech pattern," Jennet said. "That preset is so awful."

"You're just used to HANA," Tam said. "Your house is way too nice, Jennet. In all ways."

They shared a secret smile, the intensity of their feelings nearly bright enough to be visible against the shadows.

"Hi, guys," Roy called, leaning over an upper balcony Brea hadn't noticed before. "I'll be right down."

He disappeared, and she heard the thump of his footsteps,

presumably descending the stairs. A few moments later, he stepped into the hall and beckoned to them.

"I've got the theater set up for us," he said. "Oh, and welcome to my humble abode, Brea."

Tam gave a snort, and Jennet shook her head.

"Always the charming host, Roy," she said.

"It is…" Brea paused and studied what she could see of the forbidding mansion. "It is very large," she finally said.

Roy led the way deeper into the house. Although she felt the walls closing in on her, Brea forced herself to breathe normally. They passed doors on either side of the long hallway. Some were shut, and the open ones revealed glimpses of rooms—well furnished and empty.

There was no greenery adorning the interior of the house. Blessedly, there was no metal either. Their footsteps echoed hollowly off the hard stone floor of the hallway, and at last they came to a tall set of double doors.

The doors swung open at their approach, and her heart gave a startled jolt. Though she knew it was a technological power and not a magical one, the effect was still eerie. She rubbed her arms, trying to erase the chill being so deep inside the house gave her.

She stepped over the threshold, then halted in awe. True, she had seen lavish homes depicted on the vids, but they could not convey the reality of stepping into an enormous private theater. A huge screen hung from one wall, faced by rows of plush chairs.

The sides of the theater were lined with game machines, consoles, sim setups. Each area was carefully illuminated by overhead spotlights, and she could not see a speck of dust

anywhere on the equipment. It was a museum. No, a shrine—
built to honor the gods of gaming.

"We keep the FullD systems over here," Roy said, heading
toward a wall made of semi-opaque glass.

He keyed a code into the wall, and one of the glass panels
slid open. Roy and Jennet stepped through, but Tam paused a
moment, as if he, too, felt the air of reverence surrounding the
systems.

"It's something, isn't it?" he said to Brea.

"Yes."

The house, the theater in particular, was the complete
opposite of the Realm of Faerie. She sidled into the space and
studied the FullD systems displayed within. Each machine
gleamed, chrome and colorful plas-metal catching the lights.
Mounted over a section of the hardware was a low-slung
chair, with a gaming helm and gloves lying on the synth
leather.

Somehow, this equipment connected to the realm? Despite
what she had learned in the Dark Court, she still could not
fathom it.

Rough and ancient standing stones, etched with lichen and
glimmering beneath the moon, yes. An enchanted glade deep
in the greenwood, where an old oak stood sentinel and mushrooms grew in a ring, yes. Those were fitting portals to the
realm.

Yet the humans had overtaken those spaces. The stones
were in museums or private collections, the greenwood long
since cut down for lumber. Only the small places remained,
where a sprite might slip through the crack in a garden wall,

or a wisp of nightmare could linger, only to be dispelled by the dawn.

"Come here," Roy said, beckoning to her from the far machine. "I'll show you how to gear up."

Her mouth dry with fear, she joined him.

"I'll be right next to you," he said. "Don't worry."

Not trusting her voice, she gave him a tight nod. She was afraid. Of submitting herself to a machine, yes, but even more so of somehow revealing her fey nature inside the game.

Why had she so blithely assumed she was in no danger? She should never have come.

Then Roy set a reassuring hand on her shoulder, and warmth radiated from his touch.

"Hey," he said, "if you don't want to do this, just say the word."

"No... I do."

She was clever, with untold centuries of concealment bred into her very bones. Besides, she did not like to think of the Dark Queen's ire, should the monarch learn that Brea had refused a chance to observe the gateway at work. And how else would she know if her proximity to these humans, Roy especially, had made them vulnerable to the call of the realm?

She glanced to where Tam and Jennet were already gearing up with the ease of long practice, then looked again at the gaming system.

"Settle in," Roy said, picking up the helmet and gloves. "The chairs are pretty comfortable."

Brea perched on the edge of the sim chair, then let herself relax back against the synth leather.

"All right?" Roy asked.

"It is only a chair," she said—a poor attempt at humor.

Still, he smiled at her and handed her the helmet. "Make sure the fit's right. We can adjust it."

Thank the moon and stars the helm was made of plastic. She would not have been able to bear so much metal wrapping her head.

"I think it is satisfactory," she said.

"Nod your head. Now back and forth. Okay, looks good." Roy held out the heavy gloves. "The hardest part is learning how to move your character once you're in-game. Lifting your fingers, pointing, tapping your fingertips—all of those control your character."

Fear seized her again. "What if I am unable to move?"

"We'll be there with you. It's not that hard to figure out the controls, I promise." He touched her shoulder again.

That brief infusion of human energy steadied her. Had she not come, bewildered and unprepared, into the mortal world? And had she not succeeded in everything she'd set out to do, despite being alone and beset by strangeness on all sides?

She had already triumphed over greater obstacles than this. Making herself a place in the human world, navigating the intricacies of the mortal high school, even infecting humans with susceptibility to the faerie realm. Well, and so she hoped. Today might be the proof of that, and of whether she would be able to return to the realm, to her home, instead of facing banishment.

Resolutely, she pulled on the gloves and settled back into the chair.

"Can you hear me?" Roy's voice sounded in her helmet, as clearly as though he was standing beside her.

"Yes."

"We're here, too," Jennet said.

Brea could hear the smile in her voice, and her fear subsided a bit more.

"What do I do now?" she asked, lifting her hands. The gloves made her gestures heavy and awkward.

"You don't need to wave your hands around," Roy said. "The sensors will pick up small movements. Sometimes all you have to do is *think* about moving, and the interface translates the motion."

"Very well." She set her hands back down in her lap.

Her vision was overtaken by a glowing image—an expanse of white with three colorful symbols arranged in a line.

"When you see the menu," Roy said, "use your index finger to point at the *F*."

She squinted, finally making out that the middle symbol was a stylized letter F, decorated with golden scrollwork.

"Tam and I will meet you guys in there," Jennet said.

"You sure about that?" Roy's voice held a subtle warning.

"Oh. Right." Jennet was silent a moment.

"How about this," Tam said. "Me and Jennet can go check on things. Tell us when Brea's ready, and we'll come back out and let her go first."

"That should work," Roy said.

Brea paid little heed to their words. Most of her attention was taken up by manipulating a small dot of light around the menu screen. It followed the tiny movements of her index finger most obediently. When she tapped her fingertip down, the light jumped.

At length, she pointed to the glowing *F*. It was time to explore the game.

She would enter Feyland, in a strange reversal of her arrival into the human world. And hope that she would not end up trapped there, haplessly bearing the anger of the Dark Queen.

CHAPTER FOURTEEN

As soon as Brea selected the *F* icon, the sim helmet went dark. Mysterious music filtered in through the speakers and slowly a golden glow sifted across the visor screen.

WELCOME TO FEYLAND

The words rippled slightly, as if stirred by the lightest breeze. The letters flared up, bright as flame, then subsided, changing to crimson, then darkening to cinders. An eddy of wind swirled through, and the words broke apart, the pieces dancing and hovering like ashy moths.

Behind that scrim, disembodied eyes regarded her. Brea shivered—they uncomfortably resembled the slitted gaze of goblins.

The image cleared to reveal a confusing array of characters ranged before her—humans of all shapes and sizes, garbed in a dizzying number of colorful outfits.

"Are you at the character creation yet?" Roy asked.

"I believe so. How do I choose?"

She studied the titles beneath each figure. Knight and Mercenary seemed clear enough, as did Assassin. But what was a Kitsune, or a Fighting Monk, or Priest?

"Probably best for you to roll a non-melee class," Roy said. "Spellcaster maybe, or Darkmage."

"If it helps," Jennet's voice broke in, "I think we're clear to play our alts."

"Good." Roy's tone held a relief Brea couldn't decipher. "Brea, go ahead and check out the abilities of the characters and see what appeals to you."

"I shall."

She selected the Spellcaster—a woman garbed in long blue robes, holding an oaken staff with a crystal set in the top. A magic wielder seemed appropriate, but when she reached the listing of the character's spells, she balked. Lightning bolts of power were bad enough, but fireballs and sheets of flame made her skin crawl.

Fire was not her element. Indeed, she'd prefer to stay far away, even in the context of playing a game.

Darkmage was an equally poor choice. Brea did not want to call any more attention to herself from the darker half of the realm, which playing such a character would surely do.

"What do you think?" Roy asked.

"I am still pondering." It was on the tip of her tongue to ask about water creatures, yet caution held her back. Revealing too much of herself was dangerous.

Quickly, she scanned the other options. Priest was too closely aligned with powers foreign to the Realm of Faerie. Archer was an uncomfortable choice for one who had been prey much of her life. Kitsune, while intriguing, also dealt with the element of fire.

"Are there no other choices than these?" she asked at last.

"Hm." Roy was silent a moment. "Okay, try this. At the bottom right corner is a little box. Select it and see what happens."

She did, and a screen with three other characters appeared.

Necromancer—certainly not. The Sorceress seemed possible. Ah, but the last choice... She smiled and selected the Dryad. Not quite as good as a Naiad, but earth was a complementary power to water.

DRYAD: With an affinity to all living things, the Dryad possesses powerful healing abilities. She is not without resources in a fight, however, and is able to become immune to damage for twenty seconds by transforming into an oak tree. Additional offensive magic spells include Wasp Sting and Thorn Bite.

Well enough. Brea selected the character.

"I have chosen," she said.

"Excellent," Roy said. "Now customize your avatar and let me know when you're ready."

It did not take long to individualize her avatar, although Brea wished the choices for hair color were not so garish. In the end, she settled for pale silver instead of a shocking green or purple. At least the character's garb was plain enough: tunic, trousers, and boots in shades of moss and earth. She bore a short staff entwined with a living vine.

Character complete. Enter game?

"I am finished," she said.

"We're coming out," Tam said. "Go ahead and log in."

Brea's heartbeat fluttered uncomfortably fast. What would she find on the other side of the digital interface?

"How do I begin?" she asked.

"Lift your index finger to send your avatar into Feyland," Jennet said. "I can hardly wait to see what character class you chose."

Scarcely breathing, Brea moved her finger in the command to enter the game. Golden light flared across the screen. She blinked, the afterimage of brightness printed on her eyelids. A tingling sensation went through her, an effervescence, as though she were filled with carbonated water. For a moment, she felt transformed back into her essential body, shedding the awkward limbs of a mortal.

The moment passed, leaving an ache of yearning behind. She swallowed, trying to banish the taste of longing. Trying to remember her purpose.

"Tell us when you're in," Roy said.

"I am there."

Her character had materialized in the center of a faerie glade. White-barked trees surrounded her, and from the velvet-green moss beneath her feet grew a ring of mushrooms. She could feel the power of the realm pulsing through the air. Equal parts of fear and excitement vied within her, squeezing her lungs and tightening her stomach until she forced herself to take a gulping breath.

A moment later, Roy's avatar appeared beside her. He was clad in long golden robes, and had a dagger tucked into his belt beside a pointed wand fashioned of hazel wood. He turned to her and smiled.

"Thought you might go that way," he said.

"What way?" Jennet asked.

"Come in and see, laggers."

Jennet made an annoyed sound.

A figure in bright silver armor materialized in the faerie ring. Brea blinked to see that it was Jennet, looking formidable with her sword and shield. Tam was right behind her. Like Brea, he wore forest colors, but his character carried a long hunting bow and had a quiver of sharp arrows strapped to his back.

"Wow." Jennet tipped her head and studied Brea. "What character class is that? I've never seen it before."

"Dryad," Roy replied. "That last prototype FullD came loaded with a couple classes they scrapped before the beta. After your sim equip, Jennet, but before full launch, which is probably why you missed them."

"Extra character choices make things too complicated for the poor, dumb players?" Tam asked, a bite in his voice.

"Hey, VirtuMax has to consider all the angles," Roy said. "Not everyone is as elite as we are."

He said the words as a plain statement of fact, without the old arrogance that had flavored some of his pronouncements. Tam and Jennet simply nodded—confirmation enough that Brea was in talented company.

"So." Tam glanced around the clearing. "Here we are. Why am I not surprised."

"Yes." Jennet shared a look with him. "Interesting."

Roy was staring at the faerie ring, though Brea did not see what was so compelling about the white-speckled red mushrooms around them. Other than their poisonous properties.

A breeze riffled the leaves of the trees, making their silver undersides flash. Brea felt a tickle on her cheek as a stray strand of hair blew against her skin. She understood that the humans thought such sensory displays were due to the advanced tech of the game, but she knew better.

They were, somehow, in the Realm of Faerie.

Her attempts to imbue fey magic into these mortals had succeeded! Although *where* in the realm they stood, she had little notion. The Dark Queen had charged her with making players susceptible to the Dark Court—but this sunlit glade was far from the midnight shadows of the queen's domain.

"Now what?" she asked, disliking the plaint in her voice.

"Use small hand motions to move your character in the direction you want to go," Roy said. "It's safe here in the clearing, so go ahead and experiment."

Brea twitched her fingers, and her character lurched a few steps to the right.

"Try just *thinking* about moving, instead," Jennet said. "That might work better."

"Yeah," Tam added, "the gloves are pretty sensitive."

Brea imagined herself leaping gracefully forward—to find herself stumbling to the edge of the clearing and running headlong into a tree.

"I do not think I have much talent for this game," she said, tears suddenly heating her eyes. Such a foolish thing to become upset over. She could only blame her unbalanced emotions on the fact she was standing within the realm, and yet her home was impossibly out of reach.

"You'll get the hang of it," Roy said. "Turn around. That's it. Now—slowly—walk over to me."

This time, she managed to control her character a bit

better. She shot an envious look at Tam, who was leaning against a tree, arms folded in a pose of complete relaxation.

"As long as you don't get too excited and dash forward, you should be fine," Roy said.

"Yeah—charging into the middle of our enemies isn't a good strategy," Tam said.

"But even if you do"—Jennet gave her a reassuring look —"I'll be there to save you."

"And don't forget your Oak Tree skill," Roy said. "It will protect you until we can get the mobs off you."

"Mobs?" Brea asked.

"Gamerspeak for enemies," he said.

"Let's go." Tam gestured to a path leading away from the clearing.

Jennet strode forward, taking the lead. Tam fell in behind her, and Roy nodded to Brea to go next.

"I'll take rearguard," he said.

They filed into the forest. Sunlight dappled the path, and shafts of light shone deeper in, flecked with bright color as butterflies wove in and out of the beams. The breeze stirred the leaves, bringing with it a faint chiming sound.

Brea missed a step, then forced herself to keep walking. Even if she recognized some of the creatures they encountered, she must give no sign.

The chiming grew louder, and soon silvery balls of light darted through the treetops overhead. What were pixies doing here?

She glanced up at the glowing creatures, and immediately tripped. Sprawling on hands and knees on the leaf-strewn path, she heard the pixies laughing. One swooped past her face and stuck out its tongue.

"You okay?" Roy asked, giving her a hand up.

"Yes." She got to her feet and brushed the stray leaves from her clothing.

"Don't let the pixies bother you," Tam said. "They're harmless."

In direct contradiction to his words, two balls of light danced about her. One gave a sharp tug at her hair, while the other pinched her arm with sharp fingernails. Brea tried to ignore them.

"Mostly harmless, you mean," Jennet said. "They can be a pain in the—go on, shoo!"

She waved her sword at the creatures, which made them giggle even more. Brea had the uncomfortable suspicion they were planning to attack her in a swarm.

"Like a sword is any good against pixies," Roy said. "I got this."

He pulled out his wand and began to draw patterns in the air. Bright lines followed the movements of his wand. Soon, a small phoenix hovered before them, glowing gold and crimson.

"Go get 'em," Roy said, lifting his hands in a dramatic gesture.

The phoenix flapped its insubstantial wings, then dove for one of the pixies that was trying to slip into Brea's boot. The pixie let out a shriek and rocketed away, and its companions rose in a swirl. The bright bird darted among them, and they scattered and reformed again, calling out in high, clear voices that Brea suspected only she could understand.

"Sizzle! Spark! Flank the dire flame, dip and scorch!"

The pixies did not seem unduly frightened. Rather, the glee of battle filled their voices as they arrayed themselves against the phoenix.

"That should keep them distracted." Roy tucked his wand back through his belt. "Let's go."

Brea stumbled a few more times as she followed Tam down the path, and once her character got stuck in the bushes when she moved too quickly.

Roy helped her get untangled.

"You're getting it," he said.

Privately, she did not think so. She felt as ungainly as a newborn creature, trying to find its feet.

The forest thinned, and she glimpsed more and more blue sky between the pale trunks. Birdsong lilted through the air, and she smelled the smoky tang of burning wood. The path meandered out of the trees, and before her lay a wide field, spangled with poppies and cornflowers.

A cottage stood at the edge of the grass, its whitewashed walls and multi-paned windows shining in the sun. From the thatched roof a chimney poked up, sporting a lazy curl of smoke. The scene was lovely and peaceful.

Except for the ugly creature squatting on the doorstep, regarding them from dark, beady eyes. It was a hobgoblin, wearing only a stained tunic that exposed the long, matted hair covering its body.

Brea sucked in her breath as its gaze fell upon her. There was recognition in the hobgoblin's eyes, but no welcome. Indeed, a hostile light flickered, faintly orange, behind those black pupils. The creature flexed its fingers, showing dirty black claws, then grinned at her, an expression full of sharp-toothed malice.

Oh, she was in trouble, indeed.

CHAPTER FIFTEEN

Brea shivered and tore her gaze from the dark eyes of the hobgoblin, hoping her human companions had not noticed anything amiss. Despite the peaceful scene—the neatly kept cottage and meadow of colorful flowers—she felt dangerous eddies swirling about her.

"Has anyone met this one before?" Jennet asked. She sent a wary glance at the hobgoblin squatting on the step, and set one hand to the pommel of her sword.

"No," Tam said.

"Me either," Roy said. "Doesn't seem too friendly, does he?"

"He can't be *that* bad," Jennet said. "Considering where we are."

"Maybe." Tam looked at Brea, then back to Jennet. "We have a different party makeup now, though. Keep that in mind."

There were undercurrents in their words that Brea could not catch, and she did not like the brief suspicion she had seen in Tam's face. Still, how could he possibly guess her true nature?

"One way to find out," Roy said, striding forward.

"Hey." Jennet caught his arm and pulled him back. "Don't forget who wears the armor here."

"Oh, right. Ladies first." He waved her past him.

Brea trailed behind the trio, trying to keep them between her and the hobgoblin.

"Greetings," Jennet said when they arrived at the cottage's front door.

"Well met, adventurers," the creature said in a raspy, unpleasant voice. "What do you seek?"

"Far horizons," Roy said.

"Heroic quests," Jennet added.

"Answers." Tam's voice was quick and impatient.

Brea stood silent. She did not want to draw the hobgoblin's attention. Silence fell like a shadow over the meadow, then lingered, cold and uncomfortable.

"Well?" Roy turned to her. "There are no wrong answers. Just say something."

"What do you seek?" the creature asked again, this time fixing its eyes on Brea and dashing her hopes of remaining invisible.

"Home," she said at last, dismayed to hear the yearning in her own voice.

Roy glanced at her, sympathy lighting his brown eyes.

"What you seek lies beyond briar and bramble, east of the rowan and west of the night wind," the hobgoblin said. "I cannot grant it for you—but farther along the path is one who can. Now, begone."

"Are you sure about that?" Jennet asked.

The creature crossed its arms and made no response. It stared blankly into the forest, and suddenly resembled a statue rather than the sour goblin who had just been conversing with them.

"Hello?" She waved her hand before its eyes, but the hobgoblin sat, silent as a stone.

"Okay, that's weird," Roy said.

The four of them stood before the cottage doorstep a few moments, but nothing further happened.

Finally, Jennet shrugged. "I guess we keep going."

The humans set off on the path once more. Brea was reluctant to turn her back on the silent hobgoblin, but she had no choice.

"No impossible quests or weird riddles?" Tam shook his head. "I don't like it. Wish we'd played our mains, instead."

"We'll be fine," Roy said. "After all, this is the Bri—"

Tam cleared his throat loudly, cutting off whatever Roy was saying.

"Yeah, but that doesn't mean there's no trouble waiting," Tam said. "Or have you already forgotten?"

"Stop arguing," Jennet said. "We need to concentrate on whatever's ahead. Usually the game places an ambush where the path goes around those hills."

"Right." Tam slung his bow off his back and pulled an arrow from his quiver.

Jennet drew her sword and settled her shield more firmly on her arm, while Roy held his wand at the ready. Unsure of what to do, Brea gripped her staff tightly.

"To call up your spells, tap your fingers together," Roy said to her. "If one of us needs healing, you'll see yellow light flash around our character."

"What happens if you die?"

"We rematerialize at the faerie ring and have to run back," he said. "But we try not to let that happen."

She nodded her understanding, then tapped her fingers as Roy had instructed. A line of icons sprang up at the bottom of her vision. The angry-looking wasp and barbed thorn were her offensive spells. The gold and silver circles must be her healing abilities. And the tree at the end represented her ability to transform into an oak.

"I am ready," she said.

Roy gave her a look full of warmth. "I knew you'd pick this up quickly."

She was not so certain she deserved his praise, though she felt it as a flower feels the light.

"A battle will be the true test," she said.

As if her words had summoned them, five armored figures appeared on the path ahead. Their arms were long and stick-like, their spindle-jointed fingers wrapped around sharp spears. Bright, bulbous eyes regarded them from above twisted noses. Spriggans—and exceedingly unfriendly-looking ones.

"Who trespasses within our realm?" the middle spriggan called.

"Beat them back!"

"Throw them out!"

"Here we go," Jennet said, lifting her sword.

She strode forward, while Tam stayed back, arrow nocked to his bow. "I'll take the left," he said.

"Got it." Roy raised his wand. "Stay behind me," he said to Brea.

The twiggy creatures rushed forward. With a clang, Jennet deflected the first spear thrusts. Tam's arrow hummed through the air, striking one of their enemies in the shoulder. Roy's wand darted and dipped, and a bright net flew out, enfolding another.

Still, Jennet was fighting three of them by herself, her bright sword cleaving the air. She stabbed one of the spriggans in the chest, but took a vicious blow to her arm in return. Yellow light flashed around her as she stumbled back.

Roy shot a look at Brea. "Heal," he cried.

Concentrating on Jennet, Brea activated the silvery spell. Light shimmered around Jennet, and she straightened and rushed at the remaining two spriggans.

Tam continued to shoot, pushing back the first one he'd injured.

"Can't get a decent shot," he said in a low voice. "Come on, Jennet, get clear."

"I'll shove the right-hand one away," Roy said, slashing his wand through the air.

A wave of light coursed forward and hit the target spriggan. It staggered back, and Tam's arrow flew true, lodging in its chest.

Jennet ducked, swung her sword, and the final enemy let out a cry.

Between one blink and the next, the spriggans were gone.

"Are we victorious?" Brea asked, her heartbeat pounding furiously in the quiet aftermath.

"Yes." Jennet joined them.

Tam stowed his bow and arrows, then held out his hands to Jennet. "Let me see your arm."

"I'm fine." She smiled at Brea. "Thanks for the heal."

"I shall be faster, next time." Now that she understood the nature of the game's battles.

"Still." Tam leaned over Jennet's arm and ran his fingers over her smooth armor. Finally, he nodded and let go.

She gave him a quick kiss, then turned to face the path once again. "Let's go, before the game sends more creatures at us."

Brea did not relish the thought of another battle so soon, though her heartbeat was slowly calming.

"What lies ahead?" she asked, falling into step beside Roy.

"Not sure. Things change in here all the time. Probably not another fight—but be on your guard."

The peaceful rolling hills carried on serenely. Cloud shadows dappled the farther rises, and the red and blue flowers swayed under the riffling breeze. The path twisted and turned, so that they could not see too far ahead. Brea was content enough to walk beside Roy, their footsteps echoing in time.

Unexpectedly, a bright and momentary happiness settled upon her. It was not ease she felt, this breathless tingling sensation running over her skin. Perhaps it came from the magic of the realm beneath her feet. Or perhaps from striding beside this handsome human boy, whose brown eyes were deep forest pools that almost felt like home.

Absorbed in the curious sensations, she nearly collided with Jennet, who had come to a sudden stop. Roy caught Brea's arm, and his touch sent a shiver of light through her.

That light quickly faded, however, as she regarded what lay in the hollow before them. Backed up against the hillside, two standing stones rose, with a third laid across their tops. In the darkness between, she glimpsed a quick, furtive movement.

A dolmen into the hills. She could feel the Realm of Faerie in all its awful majesty, waiting within that portal. And she did not want to step any closer to it.

It was not just her fear of the Dark Queen, though Brea had successfully brought three humans to the very threshold of the realm, and the queen would be pleased.

Yet that success closed her throat and made her shiver. She did not want to give up these mortals to the dark magic of the queen.

"We should turn back," she said, touching Roy's hand.

Grief flared through her. Ah, she was the worst kind of betrayer, to lead him here all unknowing.

"Go back?" he asked. "Things are just getting interesting."

Tam turned and regarded Brea. The look in his eyes was sharp as a fishhook.

"Why?" he asked softly.

"I mislike this place. Surely we have gamed long enough?"

"Don't be afraid." Roy squeezed her hand, which only sent a renewed surge of guilt through her.

Jennet tilted her head at Brea. "Any reason why you want to stop, in particular?"

A thousand excuses rose to Brea's lips, then fluttered away. She could make no response they would believe. And if she succeeded in turning them back, there would be no escape from the wrath of the Dark Queen.

She let her fingers slip from Roy's.

"Very well," she said, though the words stung her mouth. "Let us continue."

Tam raised an eyebrow at her, then gestured Jennet forward. "Right, then. On we go."

Slowly, the four of them approached the dark depths of the dolmen. Bits of mica glittered, embedded in the rough granite. High up in the distant air, Brea heard the sound of chimes. She did not think her mortal companions could have discerned it, but Roy lifted his head a moment.

A cold breeze blew from the opening between the stones. Jennet slid her sword from the scabbard, metal hissing against metal.

"Who's there?" she called. "Show yourself."

The creature biding within let out a laugh. It echoed uncannily, and every sense urged Brea to flee. Yet whatever awaited in the shadows, she must bear the consequence. Swallowing her sorrow, Brea stood her ground, at the backs of the humans she had betrayed.

CHAPTER SIXTEEN

Heart pounding, Brea watched Jennet approach the dolmen. The dark opening between the stones pulsed with fey magic, and the air tasted of bitter pennyroyal.

Words of caution and regret seared Brea's lips, unspoken. She lifted her hand and took a step forward, though to what avail she did not know.

Too late. A cackling creature burst forth from the darkness between the stones. Brea sucked in a breath, the air whistling between her teeth.

Jennet froze, sword raised, then let her weapon drop. "Puck!" she cried.

Bright-eyed and tangled-haired, clad in leafy tatters, the sprite known as Puck somersaulted through the air. He alighted on the flat-topped stone of the dolmen and made them an elaborate bow.

"Greetings!" he said, his voice high and merry. "What an odd band of travelers I see before me."

"You've seen us plenty of times before." Tam lowered his

bow and slid his unused arrow into the quiver on his back. "You're the odd one, if I may say so."

"Am I so?" Puck looked directly at Brea, the recognition plain in his eyes.

Confusion and the heat of fear rushed through her. Would Puck reveal her true nature to these mortals? And how did they even know to name him, let alone so familiarly?

There was much here she did not understand—yet her very life hinged upon it.

"Is this a character in Feyland?" she asked Roy, attempting a tone of innocence.

"Basically." Roy's gaze shifted to the flower-specked meadow. "Puck can be helpful, but mischievous. And he always shows up unexpectedly."

"I see."

Mostly, she sensed that Roy was withholding the truth. These humans knew Puck—the *real* Puck, not some animated computer construct. Somehow, they had spent time within the Realm of Faerie. And returned, unscathed, to the mortal world.

The heat running through Brea faded, replaced by the cold certainty that the Dark Queen had left far too much unsaid about Brea's mission in the human world. And the people she might encounter—who clearly were not the unknowing innocents the queen had promised.

Ah, the ground was treacherous beneath Brea's feet. One misstep could plunge her into exile—if she survived the icy wrath of the queen.

"What do you seek, bold adventurers?" Puck asked, echoing the hobgoblin's questions.

But Brea knew the question was directed at her.

"Answers," Jennet said.

"Balance," Roy added.

"Truth." Tam folded his arms.

The humans and sprite looked at Brea.

"Freedom," she said.

How she yearned to be free of the queen's yoke, free of the sweet discomfort of Roy's presence, free of the tangle of deception wound about her. To slip beneath the still surface of a woodland pond, to feel the current caress her skin; that was all she desired.

"Hee hee!" Puck rolled backwards, then sprang up and strode upon the air as though it were solid earth. He paused before Jennet and poked her shoulder with one long finger. "You, Fair Jennet, should trust the answers within you."

"Helpful as always," Tam said. "Good to know some things never change."

"As for you, Bold Tamlin…" Puck swaggered across the open air to face Tam. "The truth is beneath your nose, as usual. Alas, that you do not recognize it."

The sprite tweaked Tam's nose, then sprang back, laughing, when Tam swiped at him.

"Royal One." Puck's smile dimmed. "A long and longer road lies before you, filled with joy and with sorrow. Only the light of a promise can guide you home."

Roy raised his eyebrow. "Cryptic."

"And not very encouraging." Jennet pushed a strand of hair behind her ear and frowned at Puck.

"My role is not to soothe and sweeten," Puck said, coming

at last to hover before Brea. "And here I find a pretty puzzle indeed. What name do you call yourself, maiden?"

Brea moistened her lips with her tongue. "I am—"

"Wait!" Roy stepped up and laid his hand on her arm. Warmth tingled out from his touch. "I'm not sure you should answer that."

"And why not?" Did these mortals know the power of naming?

Ah, she was in trouble deep. She must hope they could not parse her chosen name, and discover what she truly was.

A lark soared over the hill, its sweet melody a counterpoint to the tension winding about her. Puck regarded her with bright eyes, danger dancing in their depths like wisps of green flame.

"I think it's okay," Jennet said. "This is Puck, after all."

"Go ahead." Tam watched Brea, expression unreadable. Of the three mortals, he was by far the least trusting. She shivered, though the breeze was warm.

"I am called Brea Cairgead."

"Haha!" Puck twirled up into the air, like a reckless autumn leaf tossed by the wind. "Well spoken, Maid Brea."

Her breath spilled in a relieved rush over her lips. Her name held enough truth that Puck accepted her. She even dared hope he would not disclose her secret to the humans.

"And does Brea get an answer to what she seeks, too?" Roy asked.

Puck ceased his wild spinning. His hair was a brush of windblown tangles, bits of colorful leaves and feathers caught in the strands.

"Aye," he said. "Maid Brea, only you can choose the path that leads to your freedom."

There was no easy answer for her, and the faint flicker of hope within her chest died. It was very well for Puck to speak of choices; he was an unfettered spirit moving freely within the realm, bound to serve neither the Bright King nor the Dark Queen. But for herself, she had no choice. Freedom was an illusion.

"Well, it's been fun," Tam said. "But I think we'd better get back to questing."

Puck held up his long-fingered hand. "Best to depart altogether," he said. "The hunt is stirring, and I fear it will be able to find you even here."

With that, he gave Brea another piercing, half-accusatory glance. Then, before any of them could react, he flipped into a backward somersault and was gone.

"Do you think he meant it?" Jennet asked, her voice tight.

On the heels of her words came a low, wavering wail. The horn of the Wild Hunt.

Brea's bones nearly turned to water at the sound. Was this the queen's plan—to capture the mortals by the hunt? That fearsome gathering would not treat her well. What was one small denizen of the realm, after all? She was expendable.

"Crap," Roy said. "I just tried logging out. We're stuck."

The horn sounded again, accompanied by the first faint, high yipping of spectral hounds. Black clouds skimmed over the sky and the light dimmed.

Brea wrapped her arms tightly about herself. They were, all four of them, doomed.

CHAPTER SEVENTEEN

A COLD WIND whipped across the darkening sky, pricking Brea's skin and lodging itself in her chest. The Wild Hunt was going to capture them, and there was no escape. A faint whimper escaped her lips.

"Let's go!" Roy grabbed her elbow and spun her around on the path.

Tam and Jennet pelted past them, Jennet beckoning urgently.

"We have to make it back to the faerie ring," she said. "Quick!"

There was no time, no breath to argue. With Roy beside her, Brea ran. Despite her efforts, Tam and Jennet pulled away. She could tell Roy was deliberately slowing his pace to stay with her. Curse her inexperience with the game.

Perhaps she could delay the hunt enough for Roy and his friends to escape back through the gateway.

"Go," she gasped.

"Not without you." His voice was uncompromising.

Ahead, Jennet and Tam paused, waiting. The cottage stood behind them, gleaming white against the gray sky and deep green forest. No curl of smoke rose from the chimney, no lamplight shone from the windows, no hobgoblin squatted on the doorstep. They would find no refuge there.

"We can make it," Roy said.

Brea cast a glance behind her. The clouds roiled, lit with an uncanny blue glow. Within the billows she glimpsed the sinuous bodies of red-eyed hounds, the flashing hooves of eldritch horses. And silhouetted above them, the fearsome antlers of the Huntsman.

She stumbled, clumsy as a new fawn surrounded by wolves. Fear pinched her breath within her lungs.

"Come on!" Tam yelled.

Jennet pulled her sword from the scabbard, the metal silver-white in the eerie light.

"Hold tight," Roy said.

Before Brea could protest, he scooped her up in his arms. She did not ask how he managed to do so—in the intersection of magic and game, almost anything was possible. She laced her hands behind his neck and imagined herself light as a leaf borne across the surface of a still pond. The jostling rhythm of his steps played counterpoint to the strong pulse of his heart. He was warm, his chest rising and falling as he ran.

Tam took the lead, and Jennet closed in behind them, her expression fierce.

The light dimmed as they entered the trees, branches screening the sky and the pale trunks standing sentinel. Still, the forest offered little protection from the hunt. The sharp yipping of the hounds was audible now. Something crashed in the underbrush before them, and Tam swore.

"Jennet," he called, "get up here."

Face tense, Jennet pushed past Roy.

"Release me," Brea said, wiggling in his arms. "If a fight is ahead, you will need to draw upon your skills. And I will contribute in what small way I can."

She did not want to leave the refuge of his embrace, but it was necessary.

Slowly, Roy let her slip free. He regarded her, his brown eyes serious.

"Be careful," he said. "No matter what happens, run for the faerie ring. It will take you home."

Bitter laughter bubbled in her chest. Ah, no. The Wild Hunt would carry her home, were she captured. But the ring would take her to safety in the mortal world, if she could but reach it.

"I am not abandoning you," she said.

"You're the least experienced player," he said. "Now stop arguing, and let's go help Jennet."

Brea turned, then caught her breath when she saw what barred the pathway ahead—an elfin knight astride a flame-hoofed mount. His face was terrible and beautiful beyond measure, his pale hair glimmering, his eyes cold as the unreachable stars. Two hounds slunk before him, sharp teeth bared.

"So easily ensnared, young humans." He laughed, a cold, metallic sound. "Bide a moment here with me, until my companions arrive."

"I don't think so." Tam lifted his bow, arrow nocked.

Instead of aiming at the elf-knight, he let the arrow fly at the horse. It struck the mount's rear, and the horse gave a high-pitched neigh, bucking in discomfort.

Jennet swept her sword up in that moment and charged their enemy.

"Go, go." Roy shoved at Brea's shoulders, steering her to one side of the path.

She stumbled through the underbrush, prickly shrubs clawing at her legs. From the corner of her eye, she saw Jennet stabbing and blocking. The whir of Tam's arrows filled the air.

The two hounds lifted their heads. An arrow struck one through the shoulder and it yelped, attention drawn back to Tam, but the other fixed its red eyes upon her. The muscles gathered in its haunches as it prepared to leap.

"Look out!" Roy cried.

In the heartbeat before the hound reached them, Brea threw her arms about him and cast her spell of transformation. *Please, let it succeed.*

Thick bark rippled over her skin, encasing her—and Roy. Branches sprouted from her shoulders, and she felt her toes dig into the soil below. She could not help but be aware of Roy's body, pressed the length of hers.

"Good thinking," Roy said, his breath warm against her ear. "How long does it last?"

"Only a few moments," she said.

The hound snarled and snapped at their legs, now protected by the trunk of the tree. Brea bent, trying to lash at it with her branches. Already she could feel their protection dissolving. Another few seconds and the hound's snapping jaws would surely fasten upon her.

The branch she had been ineffectually flailing disappeared as the bark covering her and Roy peeled away. The hound flung itself forward, jaws snapping. Sharp teeth closed about her shin.

"Ahh!" she cried as white-hot pain flared from the hound's ferocious bite. She staggered, then fell, the bracken scratching her as she broke through to the damp ground.

With a curse, Roy jumped on the hound, a knife flashing in his hand. He stabbed at the hound's neck and it turned on him with a snarl.

She had no weapon but her short staff. Gritting her teeth against the pain, she rose to her knees and whacked the hound over the head. It fell back, dazed, and Roy quickly finished it off.

"You okay?" He took her shoulders and stared deeply into her eyes.

"Well enough." The searing ache in her leg spoke otherwise. "See to the others."

Jennet and Tam were not faring well against their enemy. The elfin knight was still astride, the height giving him an undeniable advantage. Tam's arrows pinged off his blue-tinted armor, and seemed merely to annoy the horse, who had only been startled by the first shot, rather than injured.

The fey steed neighed its battle cry, and the elfin knight slashed his sword down. Jennet let out a shout of pain. Blood dripped from her arm, marring the silver sheen of her armor.

"Bastard!" Tam yelled, drawing the dagger at his belt.

"Wait," Roy called. "Get ready!"

He whipped out his wand and began weaving patterns of light in the air, then flung his hands wide with a shout. An enormous golden lion appeared on the path. It opened its glowing mouth and roared.

The horse reared and whinnied, high and strange. In that moment of distraction, Tam and Jennet raced by the elfin knight. Roy swooped Brea into his arms again and sprinted for the clearing ahead.

Behind them came the clamor of pursuit: harsh yells, the yip of hounds, and the curling skree of bagpipes.

At the edge of the faerie ring, Jennet whirled, sword raised.

"Go," she cried.

Tam halted and nocked an arrow, but Roy kept going. Two more strides, and he reached the faerie ring. Brea clung to him. She drew one more breath of the air of the realm before golden light swirled around them.

Dizziness enfolded her, and she squeezed her eyes shut. The pain in her leg burned like a thousand flames, then suddenly was gone. Roy's arms fell away, and she missed his embrace with a deep, fearful pang.

She opened her eyes, to see she had returned to Roy's theater. Hands trembling, she pulled off the gaming gloves and sat, staring at the other systems. Would the others awaken, or had they fallen into a virtual, enchanted slumber? Barely breathing, she stared at their supine forms.

In the chair beside her, Roy blinked.

Oh, thank the moon and stars.

"Brea!" He lifted the gaming helm and stripped off his

gloves, then took her hands in his. "Your fingers are freezing. Are you all right? Didn't you get bitten?"

He glanced down at her leg, the one the hound had sunk its teeth into. Cautiously, she swung her foot back and forth. There was no pain.

In the other sim chairs, Tam and Jennet stirred. Tam hurriedly pulled off his gear, then went to help Jennet. Ugly smears of red stained her arm.

"I am unharmed," Brea said, "but Jennet appears to be injured."

Roy glanced over his shoulder, his expression grim. "Yeah. But let me check you, just to be sure."

"I have told you—"

She broke off as he pushed up the leg of her jeans. The feel of his hands on her skin sent a buzz of prickling heat through her. Her ears rang, as if she stood inside a tolling bell.

"Huh." He looked down at her unmarked flesh, his brows drawing together.

"As you see, I am unhurt." She reluctantly pulled her leg away. Time to deflect his suspicion. "How is it that Jennet bears injuries? Are they severe?"

Tam had popped open a compartment in the wall that held first-aid supplies, and was now cleaning the blood from Jennet's arm. Interesting, that Roy had such things near to hand.

"Not sure." Roy rose and joined Tam and Jennet. "You doing okay?"

Jennet nodded, her face paler than usual. "Nothing a little plas-skin can't cure."

Tam said nothing, his lips set in an uncompromising line.

"Need anything else?" Roy asked him.

"Got a surgeon on call?"

Brea stood, then sucked in a sympathetic breath when she saw the gash on Jennet's upper arm. The skin gaped, showing red muscle beneath, quickly obscured by welling blood.

"Just glue me up," Jennet said, voice tight.

"Only if you promise me you'll let your dad take a look," Tam said. "This needs more than an application of plas-skin."

"He won't like it," she said.

"Yeah, well, he won't like you losing your arm even more," Tam replied. "Promise?"

"Fine."

Despite Jennet's clipped tone, Brea could hear the honesty beneath. Clearly Tam could, too, for he bent over the wound, skillfully patching it back together.

"Are you often injured when playing?" Brea asked Roy. "That seems... most unusual." And obviously magical.

Roy shifted his weight back and forth. "The FullD interface is very realistic, as you saw. Sometimes players sustain what we call carry-over, when they get hurt in-game."

He shot a glance at her leg, brief confusion in his eyes. Surely he had seen the hound bite her, but there was no evidence. No carry-over.

Still, if he was not going to be truthful about the arcane powers of the game, why should she? It seemed her fey nature had kept her from manifesting her injuries in the human world. Was that vicious bite lingering at the border between worlds, ready to cripple her the next time she entered the realm? She shivered.

"Hey." Roy stepped close and put his arm around her shoulders, in a quick, comforting hug. "I know that was intense, and a little scary. But remember, it's just a game."

His voice did not carry enough conviction, but she pretended to believe him. And she did not pull away from the sweet, searing touch of his embrace. Instead, she leaned into him, letting the steady flame of his mortal heartbeat warm her.

"So," Tam said, giving Roy a pointed look. "We need to get Jennet back to her house."

Roy dropped his arm, and Brea straightened. In the absence of his touch, the air felt too cool against her side.

"Right." Roy cleared his throat. "And figure out how to get Brea home."

"I can proceed from here on my own," Brea said. It was a simple enough thing to transport herself using fey magic.

"It's not that easy," Tam said. "You have to walk, then catch two different buses."

"Ah." Brea scolded herself for the momentary lapse. She *must* remember to act human. "Which way shall I go?"

"I hate not having my car." Roy folded his arms, and then a roguish light sparked in his eyes. "Listen—I'll try and talk Tony into unlocking it for just an hour, so I can run all you guys home."

"Won't that tweak you with your mom?" Jennet asked.

"Only if she finds out. And it's not like I could be in worse trouble than I already am. Give me a minute, then meet me out front."

Tam nodded, and Roy slipped out the glass door.

"Hanging in there?" Tam asked Jennet, cupping her cheek in his hand.

She smiled wanly up at him. "More or less."

He leaned forward and brushed a kiss over her lips. The light between them flared, so bright and true that Brea had to turn her head away.

"Ok," Tam said after a few moments, "let's move." He slid his arm around Jennet, and the two of them led the way out of the theater.

Their footsteps echoed in the cold hall, and the wall sconces caused their shadows to scurry toward the ceiling as they passed. Brea drew her shoulders in. Fey magic had inhabited this place, had dwelt within the walls, leaving a residue.

She had not noticed it before, but being in the realm again had refreshed her and amplified her senses. Carefully, she opened her mouth and breathed in. The flavor was of faerie, she had no doubt, but it carried the tang of royalty.

For the first time, she wondered at Roy's name. Royal.

There were two monarchs in the Realm of Faerie. The Dark Queen and The Bright King—sister and brother, always in opposition to one another's ways. What, if anything, did one mortal boy have to do with them?

Jennet and Tam stepped into the foyer, but Brea held back. She ran one finger down the wall, wincing at the sharp prick of magic, then brought her finger to her lips. The taste was wild and hot, and stung her mouth like wasps.

Hastily, she pulled her hand away.

That was the flavor of the Bright Court, she was certain. What a strange tangle she had stumbled into, a twisted waterway where she was beginning to fear herself lost in the dangerous eddies and backwaters.

Without human hand or voice, the wide front doors swung open. Roy stood on the stoop, afternoon light touching his hair with bronze, and Brea's heart made a slow, giddy turn in her chest.

"Ladies and gentleman," he said with a bow, gesturing to the bright red grav-car at the curb, "your carriage awaits."

"Just don't let your carriage turn into a pumpkin," Jennet said. "Don't linger too long, okay?"

Brea tilted her head in confusion. Why would his car become a plant? And why not an apple? A pumpkin seemed an odd choice.

"Yeah," Tam said, once again giving Roy that look she couldn't decipher. "I don't think it's such a prime idea, taking Brea home. Maybe George can do it."

"It's fine," Roy said, a defensive note in his voice.

"Maybe it's okay," Jennet said. "Under the circumstances." She patted Roy on the shoulder. "Keep your eyes open."

"Right. And you take care of that arm. Sit in front—Tam and Brea in back."

"Of course." Tam was already ensconced in the tiny back seat. "Come on."

Brea took a breath, then exhaled, trying to make herself small so that she would not brush against the metal casing of the vehicle. Quickly, she scrambled inside, the back of her hand burning where she accidentally brushed it against the frame.

She settled into the seat and fastened the belt, clenching her teeth against the bite of the buckle. Then she tucked her aching hand beneath her good one and stared out the window, ready to endure. If only Roy's vehicle were, indeed, a carriage, pulled by horses and made of wood, with velvet-lined seats. But such things were gone and long since gone from the human world.

CHAPTER EIGHTEEN

Roy EASED off on the grav-car's speed once they flashed past the arched gateway separating The View from the rest of the town. Jennet and Tam weren't in the car any more, to tease with his mad driving. Plus he was finding his remaining passenger a little too distracting.

Brea had moved up to the front seat once they'd dropped off the others, and Roy kept stealing sidelong glances at her. The late afternoon sunlight slanted through her dark hair, giving it a silvery sheen. She sat very still, holding her arms close to her body, her knees pressed together.

"Don't worry," he said. "I'm a safe driver, despite what Jennet tells you."

She gave him a grave look from her dark eyes. "I am not concerned as to the nature of your driving skills."

What an odd way of talking she had.

"How much longer will you be here, in Crestview?" The question reminded him how little he actually knew about Brea.

And he wanted—needed—to know so much more. Did they even have a chance at being together? Did she feel that same overwhelming attraction he did whenever they were close? Who was this mysterious foreigner who was clueless about technology, who had the softest hair he'd ever touched, who made him want to paint her in swathes of light and shadow?

And kiss. He definitely wanted to kiss her unsmiling lips and coax them to curve up.

"I will remain here a small while more," she said.

Which was really no answer at all, but if she was leaving next week, he didn't want to hear about it. Because, he realized as he pulled away from a stoplight, his heart had already decided.

Whatever the world had in store for them, it didn't matter. They had that day, that afternoon, that moment.

"Mind if we take a little detour?" he asked. "I want to show you something."

"Is it safe?"

He gripped the wheel more tightly. "Do you mean, are you safe with me? Is that why you're so nervous?"

Damn Tam for his veiled suspicion, his hints that Brea should stay away from Roy.

"Not in the least."

"Should I be insulted that you don't think I'm dangerous?"

"No. You are not frightening to me. Indeed," she added in a quieter tone he had to strain to hear, "you are fascinating."

She set her hand lightly on his shoulder, and he forced his attention back to the road as the grav-car veered to the right. Everything in him pulled toward her.

"I meant," she continued, "do you face dire consequences, should you delay your return home?"

"Nothing I can't handle."

For time with her, he would risk anything.

"Very well," she said. "Where are you taking me?"

"To the park."

The still-under-construction VirtuMax Botanical Garden was way more than a simple city park, though. When the corporation had moved into Crestview and scooped up a big piece of land, part of the deal was that they'd give back by creating a public green space. His mom didn't like nature all that much, but Dr. Lassiter was smart enough to keep the city council happy and the public face of VirtuMax all shiny.

Roy navigated the back streets. The nondescript houses straggled to a halt, but the road continued into a copse of trees. The pavement widened out into a parking lot, almost completely hidden by greenery. The far end of the lot was blocked off by a high chain-link fence. Signs posted every ten feet warned that the fence was monitored and trespassers would be prosecuted to the fullest extent of the law. He didn't know about that—but with his wrist chip and Brea's guest pass to The View, he was betting the two of them wouldn't set off the sensors.

He parked, hopped out of the car, and went to open Brea's door.

"Don't worry," he said, when he saw her glancing nervously at the fence. "The gate will open for us."

"I don't see a gate."

"That's because VirtuMax is tricky. I only found out it was

here when I saw it on the plans in my mom's office. This way." He beckoned her a few paces down the fence line.

Overgrown grasses brushed the legs of his jeans, and the oily smell of warm tar wafted up from the edge of the pavement. The fence appeared to run unbroken, but he kept his eyes on the ground, looking for the white marker.

There—a pale flash, half obscured by the tangled grass roots. He reached and took Brea's hand, her slim fingers cool in his.

"Trust me," he said, then turned and walked straight into the fence.

She did not hesitate, but matched him step for step, even when it seemed that they would surely run right into the metal mesh.

A slight ripple of current tickled the hair on his arms, and then they were through.

"What was that?" she asked with a glance over her shoulder.

"VR projection and a sensory field. I figure the people working here needed a second exit back to town, but didn't want to let all the locals in. There's a bigger gate with a code to let vehicles through, but this works."

A well-worn path stretched before them through the trees. In contrast to Feyland, the few shrubs at the edges were coated with dust, and a candy bar wrapper lay discarded in the middle of the path, a discordant crumple of bright blue and red. The sounds of the city drifted in from the distance: a siren, the push and pull of traffic, the sound of metal clanking against metal.

Roy headed quickly along the path, pausing to scoop up

the wrapper and shove it in his pocket. Stupid people, littering.

He hoped they wouldn't run into anyone. Luckily, they'd be off the main path soon. As if sensing the need for caution, Brea walked silently beside him, her fingers still twined with his.

The path branched, and he led them down the smaller, right-hand fork. After a few twists and turns separated them from the main route, his breathing eased. Less chance they'd be discovered and tossed out.

An odd contentment sifted over him, like the dappled sunlight slanting in through the trees. He always felt better the few times he'd snuck into the botanical garden, but this went even deeper. The girl beside him had a lot to do with that, he suspected. He squeezed her hand, and she squeezed back, sending him the sidelong hint of a smile.

The sound of traffic slowly merged into a different noise. Brea tilted her head, her eyes widening.

"Is that...water?" she asked.

"Yup. There's a waterfall around the next bend." He'd discovered it by following the rushing sound, too.

She quickened her pace. Hands still linked, Roy lengthened his stride. The scent of damp earth rose around them, overlaid with wet greenery. They rounded the corner, and the waterfall was revealed.

It wasn't hugely tall—about a seven-foot drop from a natural granite lip down to the clear, cold pool beneath. The white spray sparkled with tiny rainbows in the sun, and ferns and mosses edged the falls and pool. A few purple and yellow flowers grew in crevices, their green leaves shiny with moisture.

Brea let out a soft sigh, then slipped her fingers free of his. She knelt at the side of the pool and dipped her hands in.

"I wouldn't drink that," he said. "No idea where this water comes from."

"It is safe enough," she said with quiet confidence. "Still, if it concerns you, I will not drink."

Instead, she lifted her cupped hands and splashed the water over her face. Droplets clung to her eyelashes, caught in her hair like transparent pearls. A trail of water slid down her neck. She smiled then, and it was like the full moon slipping out from behind a cloud.

He'd thought she was cute, but now her face held a radiant beauty that squeezed the breath from his lungs.

"Let me paint you," he said, the words out before he could call them back.

She lifted her dark eyes to his, and he saw glints of silver swimming in their depths. The last shred of caution dissolved, and he went to his knees beside her on the damp ground.

"Paint me?" Her voice was soft and quizzical.

"More than just a sketch. A real portrait." He reached and trailed his fingers along her cool cheek. "You're beautiful, Brea."

Her skin heated beneath his touch as she blushed. Before she could say anything, he bent and brushed his lips across hers. Her breath pulled in, a soft gasp of surprise.

He was ready to back away. Maybe he'd misjudged the connection between them. But she leaned forward, placing her hands on his chest, and pressed her mouth against his.

The rush of the waterfall filled him along with her kiss. She tasted like mint and starlight, fresh and somehow pure. He slipped his arms around her, and she swayed against him, their mouths melding together until he was dizzy with sensation—the misty spray, the places their bodies touched, the falling water, the heat where their lips met.

Finally they pulled apart. Roy stared at her face, needing to see her reaction, to know if she was equally dazed. Yeah, he'd kissed girls before, but it had never been like this, breathless and full of powerful yearning.

She blinked up at him, a faraway look in her eyes. Then she smiled, and he nearly tumbled backward from the brilliance of her expression. They'd both felt that kiss all the way down.

"Hey!" a voice called, breaking the spell.

Roy jumped to his feet and gave Brea a hand up, then moved to stand in front of her. His pulse revved up as a man strode down the path toward them, his blue uniform showing he was one of VirtuMax's security.

Time to find out if the Lassiter name really was as powerful as his mother believed.

CHAPTER NINETEEN

"**Y**OU KIDS ARE TRESPASSING," the security guard said. "How'd you get in here?"

"Sorry." Roy tried his best to sound humble and apologetic, though his body was still vibrating from that kiss, from Brea's distracting presence at his side. "I'm Roy Lassiter. I know we're not supposed to be in here, but…"

The guard stopped scowling.

So, his mom was right. It was amazing what the Lassiter name could do.

"I understand," he said, his gaze flicking from Roy to Brea, then back. "Still, I can't let you stay. I'm gonna have to escort you back to your car."

"Sure," Roy said.

Brea let out a disappointed sigh, and he squeezed her hand in sympathy. They'd shared a magical moment there beside the waterfall, and he wanted to stay, too. But reality had other ideas—like always.

The guard motioned them down the path, and Roy led them back to the fence.

"I won't report you." The guard gave him a pointed look. "But don't come back."

"Got it." He nodded at the man, then stepped through the VR field.

"Are you in trouble?" Brea asked as he held the grav-car door open for her.

"No. But we may not be able to visit here again for a while."

"A pity. It is a most wondrous place."

"Yes, it is." And the memory of their kiss guaranteed it always would be.

He went around to his side of the car, shaking his head. Brea talked like she came out of a Shakespearean play sometimes.

"Is your town really old?" he asked as he pulled out onto the street.

"My town?" She darted a glance at him.

"Yeah—you know, in Ireland. Is it, what, like from the 1600s?"

"It has been there for many centuries, yes."

"Sounds nice. Nothing around here is even a hundred years old. Maybe I can come visit, once you go back home."

Money was certainly not a problem, and it would give him something to look forward to. The more he thought about it, the more he liked the idea of going to see this beautiful foreign girl in her exotically ancient home town.

"Oh." She twisted her hands together in her lap. "It is rather difficult to reach."

He turned down the main street. "You managed to get here."

"Aye, but it was not without many travails."

"Well, if you decide you'd like me to visit, after you go, let me know."

He eased up on the acceleration—and his own enthusiasm. The last thing he wanted to do was tweak things up with Brea.

"I do want to see you, but…" Her voice dropped, as she turned back into the reserved, unsmiling girl he'd first met. "I truly do not think it is possible. Although I would find much joy in your company, you would not be very welcome."

"I don't think I like your family," he said. "Do you need to escape? Emigrate? Because I could help. There are laws—"

"It is not what you fear." She laid a hand on his leg, and he tried not to swerve off the road. "I suffer no abuse nor privation."

He didn't believe her, but he was hardly going to call her a liar to her face. Still, maybe he could look into expatriate asylum laws, and pass along any useful information.

"You're down this street, right?" he asked.

She jerked her head up, taking in the houses with a quick glance. "Indeed."

Then she squeezed her eyes tightly shut, her face closed in concentration.

"You all right?" He slowed the car. "Motion sick?"

She did not open her eyes, but held up one hand, fore-stalling his questions. Roy concentrated on piloting the car smoothly to the curb in front of her house.

After a few seconds, she opened her eyes.

"Better?" he asked.

She shot a quick look out the window at her house, then turned back to him. "Yes."

Feeling rather gentlemanly, he hopped out of the car and opened her door for her. There was something about her that inspired an odd sense of protection in him. Maybe it was her old-fashioned ways, but it felt natural for him to offer his hand and help her out.

The sky was fading into gray as twilight descended. The streetlight at the end of the block flickered on, casting an orange glow over the scraggly lawns.

"Is anybody home?" Roy looked at the darkened house.

A light upstairs flicked on, as if in answer to his question.

"I should go," Brea said, still holding onto his hand.

"Can I come in?" he asked. "Meet your host family?"

"Oh, no." Her voice rose with quiet alarm. "You cannot."

"Have they forbidden you to date? That's pretty tweaked."

"No...it is just, I would need to prepare for you to visit."

"Okay." He supposed he could understand that she'd want to break the news to her hosts, rather than show up at the door with some random guy. "But I'm not that scary."

"Of course not." She squeezed his hand.

That hint of smile peeped out, like a sliver of moonlight escaping the clouds. He drew her close, and she fetched up against him like a wave upon the shore. Their lips met and everything else disappeared—the fading day, the smell of car oil baked onto the pavement, the huge, empty house waiting for him on the hill.

"I must go," she said at last, pulling back and staring into his eyes.

He could get lost there, in her gaze, in her kiss.

"Yeah." It probably wasn't the best idea to stand there for ten minutes, kissing outside her host family's house. Reluctantly, he dropped his arms and released her from his embrace. "See you tomorrow."

"Yes," she said, with a breathy wistfulness in her voice. "Good night, Royal."

Normally, he hated his name. It was so pretentious. But hearing it from her lips made him straighten his shoulders. She made him feel princely—like maybe he could live up to his name after all. Like there was a hero in there, somewhere, underneath all the everyday disappointments and loneliness.

She walked through the deepening twilight to the shadowed porch. The outside light came on, and she lifted her hand in farewell, before opening the door and slipping inside.

Past time for him to get the grav-car home. He was cutting it way too close, and if his mom found out, he'd lose the car for even longer.

But remembering the splash and hum of the waterfall, the softness of Brea's lips, he smiled. No matter the consequences, it had been worth it.

Brea kept her illusion intact, though the effort made her breath come in short bursts. Only the energy from Roy's kiss enabled her to hold the façade of the house steady. He regarded it for a long moment, then slowly returned to his grav-car and drove away.

Trembling, she let the magic fade. She stood in the crumbling foundation of a house long since gone, prickly weeds brushing her jeans, litter blown into the corner.

How would she be able to maintain her deception in the face of her attraction to Roy? It was too late to keep him at a suitable distance—far, far too late. From the moment she first looked deeply into those gold-flecked brown eyes, she had been lost, though at the time she had not known it.

Now, though...

She sank cross-legged onto the weedy ground and put her head in her hands. Too many dire tales had been told through the generations, of faerie maids ensnared by mortal love. Such things ended in tragedy, for man or maiden, or both together. Never had there been a happy ending.

Yet, knowing only heartbreak lay ahead, she could not change her course. If she were doomed to a fatal love, so be it. She would not give up the quicksilver in her blood she felt at his touch, his kiss.

There beside the waterfall, she had felt more whole than she could recall. Even in her true form, weaving between the silken, watery shadows, loneliness had been a cold companion. With him, either world became glorious.

She and Roy might have only a brief, shining burst of flame, but she vowed to make it burn brighter than the sun.

CHAPTER TWENTY

THE DARK QUEEN paced beneath an endless midnight sky. Her gossamer gown swirled like smoke in her wake, and the strange denizens of her court crouched in the tattered shadows, wary.

Wraithlike maidens with gossamer wings hovered behind the queen's throne of tangled vines. Even the mad-dancing spriggans and bogles about the violet-hued bonfire had paused, eyes glinting with eerie reflected flames.

The queen's impatience had not yet sharpened to lethal anger, and so the court waited, watching to see what course she might take. Some, like the pale water sprites and lesser hobgoblins, poised themselves to flee, should the queen's mood worsen. They had not power enough to withstand the killing frost that would fill the Dark Court at her displeasure.

"Why have no innocent mortals yet stumbled into my realm?" the queen asked the cold night. "My plan was sure."

From the side of the clearing, Bard Thomas stepped forward.

"My lady." He bowed, and the guitar slung across his back vibrated, strings stirring at the motion. "Do recall that time in the mortal world moves differently. I am confident that your... emissary is performing her task to the best of her abilities."

A clump of nearby goblins laughed at his words, the sound rough-edged and ugly.

"That one?" The leader of the goblins grinned, showing sharp teeth. "She scarcely has the power to hold her own shape, let alone send humans through the gateway."

"Indeed?" The queen's voice was icy. "Do you disagree with my actions, Codcadden?"

She strode up to the goblins, her eyes storm-deep, her face alight with terrible beauty.

Realizing his mistake, the goblin fell to his knees. "Oh no, majesty. I would never—"

"Do you think a different creature would find more success? Something fearsome and wicked? A goblin, perchance?"

Codcadden trembled and cowered on the velvet-green moss.

"My queen." Thomas inclined his head, his eyes both wise and weary. "In this instance, patience may be the better course."

"Patience!" Her voice cracked through the air, and ice formed on the branches of a nearby oak, the crystals sparkling in the moonlight. "Bard Thomas, your counsel is not always what I might wish. Are you certain you hold the interests of the Dark Court above that of the mortal world?"

"I am sworn to your service." He went on one knee before

her. "I could no more lead you astray with my words than the stars could change their course across the sky."

The queen regarded him a moment more, frost settling on his shoulders and dusting his gray-brown hair with silver.

"Rise, Thomas," she said. "Yet I shall wait no longer for the girl to succeed. Codcadden, I accept your offer to enter the mortal world to assist the little fish in her quest."

"But... milady!" His yellow eyes widened in fear. "As leader of the redcaps—"

"You have the power and cunning to succeed." The queen tilted her face up to the moon. "I shall give you seven days, until next the mortal moon waxes full. Now, name your lieutenant."

Codcadden slowly rose to his feet and surveyed the other goblins. Some of them bared their teeth, others shuffled their clawed and filthy feet.

"Goblot," the lead goblin said at last. "But don't you be thinking to usurp my place, or I'll have your head on a platter when I return."

The other goblins cackled.

"Savor his eyes as a rare delicacy," one called.

"Crunch his teeth between your own," said another.

The goblin called Goblot nodded, though a sly gleam had come into his eye. "I'll hold your place well for you, Codcadden."

"You." The queen beckoned to another of the goblins, a spindle-legged fellow with lanky black hair lying sparse upon his head. "Come thither."

"My queen?" He shuffled forward.

The queen drew a long black thorn from the sleeve of her

gown. The point was sharp enough to prick air and part breath from body in a single stab.

"I weary of sacrificing my handmaidens," she said. "Today, we shall test the strength of goblin blood."

The goblin shrieked, the sound cut off abruptly as the queen's thorn pierced his chest. Quickly, the Dark Queen wove her spell, and a sphere of eerie blue light formed beside the fallen body. The pale glow illuminated the sorrow on Bard Thomas's face, the eagerness in Goblot's eyes, and the fear in Codcadden's.

"I send thee forth," the queen said, pointing her thorn at Codcadden. "Return at the full of the moon, victorious—or not at all. And bring the fish-girl with you. Begone!"

The echoes of her shout shook the branches of the moon-silvered oaks and caused the denizens of the Dark Court to flinch. The blue light flared, outlining Codcadden's twisted shape. Then it was gone, taking him from the realm into the mortal world.

The queen nodded and tucked her thorn back into her sleeve.

"Music," she said, waving at Thomas.

Face set, he unslung his guitar and began to pluck out a melancholy air. The notes hung in the air like pale moths, swirling about the queen as she ascended her tangled throne. She sat and accepted a silver goblet from one of her gossamer-winged attendants.

Creatures crept from the shadows, ready to return to feasting and dancing now that their queen's temper had settled. A flute joined the melody, twining about the guitar notes. Then a drum, lifting the beat to a faster pulse.

Somber, all but forgotten, the remaining goblins towed the body of their fallen comrade away.

———

Roy sat up, blinking against the darkness of his bedroom. The sheets were wound around his sweating torso, and his heart raced from the nightmare that had woken him. He breathed, in, out, in, listening.

No strangeness broke the night, no wailing cry of hunting horns, no baying of spectral hounds. Yet the back of his neck prickled with danger.

On the table beside the bed, his messager dinged. Roy plucked the sheets away, then scooped it up, squinting at the screen. It was just after 5 am, and he had a group chat invite from Tam and Jennet.

:You awake?: Jennet's message blinked up at him.

:Yeah,: he typed. *:Nightmare woke me. You too?:*

:More than a nightmare,: Tam wrote. *:Something's up.:*

Roy rubbed at his face, trying to erase his unease.

:I'll go check it out. Unless you guys...?: He didn't think Tam was in the habit of spending the night at Jennet's, but she had two FullD systems. *:Might be safer with two.:*

:I'm at home.: Tam sent a frown along with the words.

:We've got to get you a sim setup,: Jennet wrote.

:I don't want Feyland anywhere near my little brother,: Tam replied.

Roy couldn't blame him. Tam's brother, affectionately called Bug, had spent days trapped in the Dark Court, a hostage of the queen. Since they'd rescued him, he'd been a bit strange. Well, stranger than he'd already been. Fey-touched, Jennet said.

:I'll go in,: Roy wrote.

:Me too,: Jennet typed. *:We'll take a quick look. I don't think you should go alone.:*

Tam stayed silent. Roy could tell he didn't like it, but he knew the dangers as well as Jennet.

:Your shoulder ok?: Roy asked.

:Good enough,: Jennet replied.

:Her dad made a med team come check on her,: Tam wrote. *:It should heal cleanly.:*

:I'm fine.:

:Ok,: Roy sent. *:Meet you in-game in five.:*

:See you in there.:

:Be careful,: Tam finally wrote, before signing out.

Yawning, Roy got out of bed and pulled on a pair of jeans and a sweatshirt. He grabbed his messager and by its soft illumination made his way down to the theater. Best not to wake his mom, though she would buy the excuse that he couldn't sleep and was going to game for a bit. Too bad she didn't accept his art nearly as easily.

Fingers still waking up, he pulled on his sim gear and chose his main character, then entered the game.

Golden light swirled around his senses, and he clenched his jaw against the dizziness. As it cleared, he saw Jennet's blue-robed Spellcaster waiting for him in the faerie ring.

"That was fast," he said.

"Well, I don't have to go three miles to get to my game room," she said.

He shrugged in agreement. Jennet's house was big, but it didn't compare to the Lassiters' mansion.

Though the clearing felt as peaceful as ever, with the soft wind playing through the pale-trunked trees, something felt off. He turned slowly, taking a closer look. The ring of mushrooms seemed slightly droopy on the side that faced the Dark Realm's clearing.

Feeling like he'd swallowed a rock, Roy stepped over to the edge of the ring. A faint smear of oily green marked a few of the mushrooms. He went down on one knee and touched the substance with one gloved finger. It didn't spark or hiss or fizzle. In fact, it faded before his eyes.

"What is it?" Jennet asked, leaning over on her staff.

"No idea—but there's a few more drops on the other side."

Jennet hopped over the ring and bent down, studying the flower-flecked mosses. "And they're starting to disappear. But they lead to…"

She turned, her face grim. Roy felt the same way. The trail led directly from the clearing where they stood to the mirror-image glade housing the Dark Realm's gateway.

A twig broke with a sharp snap, and something moved in the shadows beyond the clearing. Heart thumping, Roy drew his sword and held it, two-handed, in front of him. Jennet gripped her staff, the blue crystal set at the end beginning to glow.

He really hoped the two of them could face down whatever was coming.

CHAPTER TWENTY-ONE

Roy SHIFTED, trying to find solid footing on the soft mosses of the faerie ring clearing. The gentle sunlight and birdsong sifting through the forest only underscored the ominous shiver running down his spine. He gripped his sword tightly, and waited.

Two figures appeared between the tall pines flanking the Dark Realm's clearing. Roy hoisted his blade, ready to charge. From the corner of his eye, he saw Jennet raise her hands, preparing to send a fireball at their enemies. But something made him hesitate.

Those weren't the silhouettes of spriggans or ogres or any fey creatures. In fact, they appeared very human.

They stepped forward into the glade, and Roy let out a quiet breath. He kept his sword up, though. While the magenta-haired girl carrying a bow, and the stealthy-looking Saboteur behind her *looked* like their friends, the fey folk were full of trickery.

"Spark? Aran?" Jennet asked.

The girl smiled broadly. "Jennet! Roy—good to see you guys." Then her expression sobered. "Bet you felt that disturbance."

"We did." Roy eyed them suspiciously. "How'd you two get in here so quick?"

"Spark's on tour in Asia," Aran said. "We were in-game when things went tweaked for a second, and we came right here."

"Something got through?" Jennet asked.

"Looks like." Spark glanced at the ground. "The trail is already fading, though. We followed it a ways, back toward the Dark Court."

"Was the code changed?" Roy asked, finally lowering his sword.

Aran shook his head, his dark hair brushing his cheekbones. "Nobody's hacked it, and the gate is still closed. But the queen has other ways of getting people in and out."

He should know. Like Tam's brother, Aran had spent time in the Dark Court—though his stay had been a bit more voluntary. Roy still didn't trust him completely. But Spark did, and that would have to be enough.

"Any idea about what's now running loose in the mortal world?" Roy asked. He sheathed his sword, but didn't fully let down his guard. Anything could leap out at them.

"Aran thinks it's a goblin," Spark said. "Given his former experiences."

"Yeah—probably a redcap." Aran frowned. "A few of those guys have been through before. Easier for the queen to send one of them."

"More resonance." Jennet nodded. "Creatures that have

been in contact with the mortal world will have a connection, however faint."

It made sense. And it made sense that the queen would transport one of her more vicious subjects. Redcap goblins were nasty creatures.

"What does it want, though?" Spark asked. "How can one goblin open the gate?"

"It can't, by itself." Jennet glanced at Roy. "But something more is going on. What if it had an ally—another fey creature working for the Dark Queen—already in the mortal world?"

"What are you suggesting?" Roy glared at Jennet.

"You know." She folded her arms. "There's somebody new in Crestview who isn't what she seems."

"Brea is not a creature of the Dark Court! How could you even think that?" His pulse beat in his ears, a quick, irritated rhythm. "She might be a little odd, but she's not some minion of the queen. No way."

"Who's Brea?" Spark asked, looking from Roy to Jennet.

"An exchange student from Ireland," he said.

"A girl who's a little too mysterious and has more than a touch of the fey about her," Jennet added. "Roy, I know you like her, but you're being blind here. There's too many things about her that just don't add up. The way she talks—"

"Her village is old-fashioned. She told me so."

"She'd never gamed in her life! Nobody is that old-fashioned. Wake up, Roy."

"You're just—"

"Hey, ease it down." Spark stepped forward, her hand lifted. "Clearly you two need to talk more about it—but this isn't the place."

She shot a glance over her shoulder, at the thickening shadows in the Dark Realm's glade.

"Fine." Roy scowled at Jennet. "We'll be at school in less than two hours."

"I want Tam involved in this conversation, anyway," Jennet said. "Marny, too."

"Maybe she'll talk sense into your tweaked head," Roy said.

"Work it out," Aran said. "And let us know if you need us. We may be half a world away, but Feyland is everywhere."

"Which is going to be a problem," Spark said. "VirtuMax is really pushing this worldwide launch."

"We know." Roy glanced at his feet. It wasn't his fault his mom was the CEO, but he still felt guilty about it.

"There's been no indication of anything severe from the Elder Fey," Jennet said, though she didn't quite sound convinced.

Spark and Aran exchanged a look.

"Maybe," Spark said. "Anyway, we need to get back. Stay in touch, all right?"

"We will," Roy said.

"You two take care," Jennet added.

"And you guys be careful." Spark gave them a keen-eyed glance. "Especially you, Roy."

"Right."

But it was too late where Brea was concerned. Maybe she was somehow connected to the realm—but he just couldn't believe she was an agent of the Dark Court.

What felt like moments later, Roy's alarm sawed jaggedly through his sleep. Groaning, he turned over and whacked the snooze. He'd lain awake for too long after logging out of Feyland, turning Jennet's accusations around and around in his head.

Dammit, he'd kissed Brea. There was nothing sinister about her. Mysterious, sure. Magical, yes. If he really made himself look at the evidence, he had to admit she could be a faerie. But she wasn't evil. She couldn't be.

There was a sweet purity, an innocence about her, that couldn't be faked.

You've been wrong before, his conscience reminded him.

Okay, he had. But this was different. He just had to convince his friends that Brea wasn't a minion of the queen.

The ride down to Crestview High in Jennet's chauffeured car was silent. She kept glancing at him, but they were hardly going to start discussing how Roy's new girlfriend was probably not human in front of George, the driver.

When they arrived at school, Marny and Tam were waiting out front. Neither of them looked very happy. Tam, he could understand, but Marny? With a sinking sensation in his gut, Roy trailed over with Jennet.

Luckily, the bell for first class would ring in about five minutes, so they couldn't get too deep into who or what Brea was. He cast a glance at the students thronging into the school, hoping to find her. Although there were plenty of girls with long, dark hair, and even a couple wearing gray sweaters, none of them were Brea.

"What's up?" he asked, trying to sound cheerful, though the grim look on Tam's face was hard to ignore.

Marny crossed her arms. "I'll tell you what's up. I talked Tam into walking past Brea's house this morning."

"And? Was she there?"

"No." Tam crossed his arms. "She wasn't there. But even more important, neither was the house."

"But I dropped her off last evening and watched her go in." He matched Tam's stare. "Are you saying it somehow got demolished overnight?"

"More like twenty years ago," Marny said. "There's nothing in that lot except a crumbling foundation and a bunch of weeds. Oh, and one other thing."

"We're pretty sure we saw a redcap goblin there," Tam said.

"What?" Roy's heart gave a painful thud. So, Aran had been right.

"It was using concealing magic, but I glimpsed it creeping around the foundation," Marny said. "And there's only one place those nasty guys come from."

"Which makes me wonder," Tam said, giving Roy a pointed look, "about a certain exchange student you've been spending time with."

Roy took a step back. "Not Brea. Just because a goblin was sniffing around doesn't mean there's a connection."

"I knew it." Jennet gave a grim look. "From the second I met that girl, I knew there was something off about her."

"She's not from the Dark Court."

"At least you admit she's not a normal human girl," Tam said.

Misery coiled up from the soles of his feet. "I didn't say that."

But the evidence was mounting against Brea. If only she'd show up, he was sure she could explain. Somehow.

"There's the bell," Marny said. "Your faerie girlfriend better be there at lunch to give us some answers."

"She's not going to be," Tam said. "She knows we're on to her."

"Then we should go find her," Roy said. "If there's a goblin out there, she's in danger."

Jennet shook her head at him. "They're working together, Roy."

"If you're right…" He swallowed, tasting dust. "We should all go. She and the goblin are a threat that can't be ignored."

"Right," Marny said. "We can start at the fake house, and search from there."

Tam hefted his pack onto his shoulder. "Too bad we don't have a faerie-detection potion or something."

"I don't know of any charms like that," Jennet said. "Only things to ward off the fey folk, or dispel their glamour. I could get George to run me home and get the last bit of the faerie ointment. I'll tell him I forgot something for school."

"Do that," Tam said. "When you get back, we'll head out."

Roy nodded. His stomach knotted at the thought of Brea. Had she really been deceiving him all along? It wouldn't be the first time he'd fallen, hard, for faerie trickery. He owed it to his friends—and himself—to admit he'd been wrong. Time to let his head rule, and not his stupid human heart.

Half an hour later, they stood in the middle of the vacant lot where Brea's house had been. Or the illusion of her house.

"Here." Jennet rummaged in her satchel and pulled out a jar containing a few drops of liquid. "There's even less faerie ointment left than I remembered. Probably only enough for two of us."

"No, thanks," Marny said. "Give it to Roy."

"Roy and Tam, then," Jennet said. "That work for everyone?"

"Fine." Roy stood still, obediently closing one eye as Jennet dabbed some oil on his lid.

She did the same to Tam, then stepped back.

"See anything?" she asked.

Tam opened his eyes and squinted around the ruined foundation. "Everything looks normal."

"Yeah." Roy turned a slow circle. "Wait—something's glowing over there."

He led them to the corner of the foundation, where a faint smudge of green shone.

"Yeah," Marny said. "That's where the goblin was."

"How did you even see it?" Jennet asked.

"Well, you doused me in enough of that faerie oil a couple months ago. Maybe some of it stuck."

Roy examined the sickly glow. It was just like the green drops he and Jennet had seen the night before in Feyland. Goblin, for sure.

"It doesn't lead anywhere," he said, bending over to examine the residue. There was no trail, no other trace of the green except at that one corner.

"Spread out," Jennet said. "Check the perimeter."

A few minutes later, Tam waved from the sidewalk. "Something different here," he said. "See it, Roy?"

Roy narrowed his eyes, and could just make out a silvery sprinkle leading from the edge of the concrete into the weeds.

"Yeah," he said. "I think this is Brea's mark. This would be about where her front door was." And where they stood and kissed goodbye. His heart lurched at the memory.

"Anything else?" Jennet asked.

"Let's check one more time," Tam said, striding to the edge of the lot. "If we can't pick up a trail here, maybe we can track Brea back from school."

But, despite faerie ointment and determination, the next few hours of searching yielded only a faint dusting of silver about the hallways of Crestview High. After their second warning to get back to class, they had to admit defeat.

Exchanging looks, they slipped out onto the scrubby grass surrounding the school. It was close enough to the end of the day they wouldn't get in trouble, as long as they kept a low profile.

"We have to get in-game," Roy said. "Maybe we can find Puck and get some clues, since the Elder Fey clearly seem uninvolved."

"Either they trust us to handle it, or they're oblivious," Tam said.

Jennet pressed her lips together. "You know my dad won't be happy about me going back into Feyland until my shoulder's fully healed."

"We'll talk him around," Tam said.

"Want me along?" Marny asked.

Roy looked at her in surprise. "You'd actually sim with us?"

"No. But there's plenty of real-world fey action going on, and you know I'm good at handling stuff on this end."

"Actually…" Tam made a face. "I can't play right now. We have a family counseling session this afternoon, and I can't miss it."

Roy glanced at him. Tam didn't talk about his family dynamics much, though Roy had the sense that things were starting to get better. Still, they all knew how fragile Tam's mom was.

Jennet slipped her arm around Tam's waist and leaned into him. "It's okay. It'll take me a while to convince my dad, anyway. You know how he is."

The shrill call of final bell echoed inside the school.

"All right," Tam said, giving Jennet a squeeze and then stepping back. "I gotta go. I should be done by 4:30."

"I'll have George come get you, and Marny too," Jennet said. "If that works?"

"Fine by me," Marny said.

"Speaking of your chauffeur…" Tam tipped his head toward the curb, where the sleek black grav-car had pulled up.

"All right, see you soon," Jennet said. "Coming, Roy?"

"Yeah, thanks." He hated not having his own transpo. And at the rate he was going, he wouldn't get his car back for months.

When the door slid closed, he turned his face to the window, trying not to see the pity in Jennet's eyes. She was quiet for most of the ride up to The View, but when they whooshed under the arch, she patted his arm.

"I'm sorry about Brea," she said.

"Me too." The thought of her scratched him like sandpaper rubbed on bare skin.

"Maybe we'll find her, in-game."

"Maybe."

The grav-car pulled into his looping driveway, and Roy was glad the conversation was over. As soon as the door opened, he stepped out.

"Good luck with your dad," he said.

She made a face. "At least he knows Feyland is real. He'll come around. See you in-game about quarter to five."

"Right."

Not that he really believed they'd find Brea in Feyland. As the car pulled away, he lifted a hand in halfhearted farewell, feeling like all the light had gone out of his world.

CHAPTER TWENTY-TWO

BREA HID in the small yard separating the Lassiters' immense garage from their even more enormous house. For hours she had bided there, weaving a cloak of shadows about herself, crouching against the roughly plastered outer wall, or lying concealed beneath the juniper shrubs. Waiting for Roy to return home. She did not know how much aid he would give her, but he was her last hope.

Despite the infusion of energy from Roy's kisses, playing the game of Feyland—and especially setting foot back in the realm—had taxed her. After Roy had bidden her farewell at her faux home, she'd fallen asleep in the ruins, only waking as dawn crept into the sky.

With a flash of starlight and a shimmer of water, she had transported herself back to her shelter in the Exe.

The faerie protections she had set about the place glowed a sullen red against the dim sky, a sign that an intruder had found her refuge. And not any intruder—a denizen of the

Dark Court. Heart fluttering in her chest, Brea crept closer. The rank smell of goblin singed her nose.

Carefully, she peeked through one of the holes in the crumbling walls, to see a fierce redcap squatting among her things. Her velvet coverlet and soft clothing had been shredded by his long, dirty claws, her cosmetics upended, her chain of crystals smashed—all her tenderly gathered possessions in ruinous disarray.

Anger heated her breath, and she must have made some small noise, for the goblin looked up, yellow eyes glinting. With dismay, she recognized him as Codcadden, leader of the fearsome redcaps, and a vicious goblin indeed. She could guess why he had come to the mortal realm, and it boded ill for her.

"Come out, pretty fish," he said, his mouth stretched into a leering grin. "I promise not to eat you, though you would be a tasty thing grilled over a fire."

She shuddered, trying to control the fear clamoring in her head. There was only one precious thing remaining within her ruined haven. The enchanted chest holding her medallion.

Striving to remain as motionless as possible, she scanned the debris of Codcadden's ransacking. At last she spotted the chest, tilted on one side amid a heap of litter and rubble. It appeared the goblin had tossed it aside, thinking it of no value. Brea closed her eyes in brief thankfulness that the spells protecting the chest and its contents had proven true.

"Why so shy?" the goblin called again. "The queen has sent me to help you. Together, the two of us should be able to infect a score or more of the humans before the moon brims full. Won't we have fun?"

Codcadden chuckled. Faster than Brea could react, he sprang over the wall and caught her arm in a tight grip. The stench of him made her eyes water, and she flinched away, trying in vain to pull from his grasp.

"You cannot hide," he said. Still grinning, he brought her hand up to his grotesque face, then stuck out his black, slimy tongue and licked the inside of her wrist. "Delicious."

"Let me go," she said, shuddering at the feel of his spit sliming her skin.

"Not until you agree to work with me, tricksy girl."

"I do," she said, and felt his fingers loosen. "Not!"

She tore from his grip and, barely thinking, folded air and space about herself. It was dangerous, to flee without a clear sense of direction, but she must escape Codcadden.

Ears ringing, she stumbled and fell to her knees. After a few deep breaths, blessedly free of goblin stench, she raised her head and recognized where she had come. Roy's house.

Difficult for the goblin to track her there, but not impossible, especially with his spittle still greasy upon her arm. She could not wipe it upon the green grasses, no matter how she burned to remove that disgusting touch from her skin.

Using the last of her magic, she wove a cloak of shadows, then stole up to the front of the house. The fountain splashed, the droplets crystal clear in the light of the new sun. From the white marble basin, the nixie regarded her, unblinking. Her long, pale arms were folded along the edge of the basin, and her weedy green hair swirled in the water.

"Pardon, nixie, for the intrusion," Brea said, choosing her words with care. "I beg a boon of thee."

"No boon comes without price," the creature said, her

words high and burbling, almost indistinguishable from the plash of the water.

"The payment is the deed itself." Brea held up her soiled arm. "A bit of goblin spittle to weave into your protections and enchantments. You may keep it all, in exchange for washing me clean."

The nixie narrowed her cat-slitted eyes. She plunged beneath the water, flicking up a jet of spray. Brea waited, trying neither to hope nor despair. The sun glinted off the water, and around her filtered the sounds of the human neighborhood awakening. She could not linger too long before the fountain, or she would be spotted.

Just when she turned to leave, the nixie reemerged. Water streamed from her hair. She held up one web-fingered hand, displaying a triangular bottle.

"I accept your offer," she said in the hiss of spray and lap of wave.

Relief weakened Brea's knees. She laid her arm along the fountain's edge, and the nixie positioned the bottle beneath. With a wiggle from those blue-tipped fingers, the goblin's spit slowly ran down Brea's arm and into the mouth of the bottle.

The nixie bobbed close and examined Brea's skin, sniffing from wrist to elbow with her flat nose. With a satisfied slap of water, she corked the bottle, then sent a rivulet from the fountain splashing over Brea's arm.

It was a blessing to have the foul stuff removed from her skin—and to know that Codcadden could no longer hunt her down quite so easily.

The sound of an engine nearby recalled Brea to her

danger. She made the nixie a formal, courtly bow, then scurried for the shadows beside the Lassiters' garage.

Royal's mother exited the house moments later, looking stern and stiff in a coat and skirt the color of night. A car took her away, and Brea crept to the corner of the house. Surely Roy must emerge soon.

The sun ticked higher, and a sleek black grav-car pulled into the looping driveway. It gave a sudden blare, and the back door slid open. Brea caught a glimpse of pale blonde hair within, and shrank back into the prickly juniper. The house's front doors swung wide, and Roy rushed out, stuffing his tablet into his backpack.

Before Brea could do anything to catch his attention, he hopped into the back seat of the car and the door closed. The driver pulled smoothly away from the curb, and her chance was gone.

And so she waited, as the shadows crawled across the manicured lawn. Once a passing feline paused, then sat and stared at her until it decided she was of no interest. Twice, the nixie allowed her to drink from the fountain.

At last, the black grav-car returned and Roy got out.

"Good luck with your dad," he said to someone inside the car.

Jennet answered, and Brea shrank back into the shadows. The only human she could trust was Roy. She waited until the car hummed away, then softly called his name as he strode toward his house.

He stopped and lifted his head, then shook it and continued along the walkway. The huge double doors of his entry swung open.

"Royal." She let go her cloak of concealment and stepped forward.

"Brea!" He whirled to face her.

The expression on his face was not delight; his brown eyes were guarded, his mouth set. Nonetheless, he was her last hope of refuge.

"I need your help," she said.

The bushes rustled behind her, and she shot a wary glance over her shoulder. Only the wind. Still, her heart galloped like a racing horse. She took a cautious step forward, wishing Roy would open his arms and welcome her into his embrace.

Instead, he folded them. "I have one question for you. Answer it with the truth."

His voice cracked on the last word, and he glanced away for a moment. Beneath his cold exterior, she glimpsed a flash of despair.

"Ask me your question." Premonition shivered over her.

Somehow, the humans had discovered what she was. His next words confirmed it.

"Are you from the Dark Realm?"

Though it tore her heart to say it, she must answer him true. "Yes. But—"

"No excuses." He slashed his hand down, his voice hard. "The Bright Court is bad enough, but this... Just, no."

She took a few trembling steps forward, until they stood face to face. His eyes were bright with pain, and she wished she could soothe it away.

"How do you and your friends know so much of the Realm of Faerie?" she asked.

"We've been there—in both courts. I'm surprised the queen didn't fill you in. She's tried to kill us a number of times, now."

Curses upon the sly and subtle monarch! Ah, if only Brea had known the truth, how things might have been different. But it was too late now. Might-have-beens faded like moonbeams under the harsh light of day.

"I never meant to harm you." Brea held her hand toward him, palm up.

He seized her hand, gripping it as though she were a lifeline in a turbulent storm. "Dammit, Brea. I trusted you. I…"

Again he looked away. After a tight breath, he dropped her hand.

"As Feyguard, it's my job to send you back to the realm."

Icy fear flashed through her. "No—there is only exile and sorrow awaiting me there."

"I don't want to hear about it. You don't belong here, Brea. And whatever you've been doing, it's time to put an end to it. I need to message Tam and Jennet."

Then she would be truly outnumbered, with no hope of an ally. And she had no doubt they could find some means of returning her to the Dark Court.

"Please, Royal—"

"No." He slung his pack off his shoulder and began rummaging through the contents.

"But I can aid you." Desperation nearly stole her breath. "The queen sent a fearsome goblin through—"

"We know. We'll deal with him, too." He pulled out his messager.

A single tear rolled down her cheek and fell, glistening,

onto the perfectly trimmed grass. The nixie watched silently from the fountain. No help would come from that quarter.

No help would come from anywhere.

"Farewell," she whispered, before folding the light and air about herself once more.

"Brea, no!" Roy lunged toward her, but she was already gone.

She ached inside, with a fierce burning as though a piece of her heart had been ripped away to stay behind with him. Forever.

CHAPTER TWENTY-THREE

Roy's fingers passed through the shadowy form of Brea as though she were mist.

"No!" he cried, but it was too late. She'd disappeared, and he had no way of finding or following her.

Dammit, why hadn't he thought it through? She was magic. Of course she wouldn't just stand there while he called in the rest of the Feyguard. He was an idiot, on so many levels.

Grief and loneliness ripped through him. He had to go inside, meet the others in-game and tell them what had happened. After he got hold of his emotions. The lump of shame and sorrow in his throat made it hard to breathe, let alone talk.

He'd been so wrong.

And now he and the rest of the Feyguard had to hunt down Brea and the goblin. *The Dark Court creatures*, he reminded himself. She might not be a goblin, but she was no better than one.

Something sparkled in the grass at his feet—a smooth, teardrop-shaped crystal. The memory of Brea's sorrow.

He bent and picked it up, folding it into his palm. Maybe she had cared for him, too—if the fey folk had such emotions. It warmed under his touch, then nearly scorched him, hotter than his skin. Roy opened his fingers, to see the teardrop glowing. In the depths, as though it were a tiny crystal ball, was the figure of Brea. His heart gave a thump at the sight of her—and her surroundings.

She was in the Exe.

Roy raised the crystal, his heart beating faster as he watched the image inside. There was no mistaking the graffiti-etched walls and crumbling sidewalks surrounding her. A dead tree reached into the sky, branches covered with brown, desiccated leaves. Brea crouched behind the rotting trunk, then slowly peeked out.

Nearby lay a tumbled shelter filled with torn clothing and overturned possessions. And a redcap goblin.

He squatted in the cluttered mess, holding a rat in his filthy claws. As the rodent twitched, the goblin opened his mouth and bit down, sharp teeth severing the rat's head from its body. Blood spurted out, covering the goblin's chin, and the cap on his head turned a brighter red. The goblin gave a gruesome smile, and Roy swallowed back his rising bile.

Within the crystal, the tiny figure of Brea shuddered, then retreated, away from the tree and into the shadows of a sordid alley. She picked up a hunk of concrete and weighed it in her hands. She hefted it, frowned, and set it back down. As the vision faded, he saw her grab a shard of glass.

The teardrop cleared, sparkling innocently in the sunlight.

Ah, crap.

If what Roy saw was true, Brea and the goblin weren't allies. And she was looking for a weapon.

She couldn't be planning to attack it by herself. Damn stupid faerie. Whatever Brea *was*, behind the façade of a mortal girl, he'd bet she was no match for a redcap goblin.

And he couldn't deny he still cared for her. He couldn't stand by, knowing she faced her death. Fear and hope raced through him, and he tucked the crystal in his jeans pocket. If it heated up with another vision, he'd feel it through the cloth.

He scrabbled in his pack for his messenger.

:Jennet, you there?:

No answer—maybe she was in the bathroom or something. But he didn't have time to sit around and wait for her to answer. Tam was unavailable. Maybe Roy could track down Marny, but she could be any number of places. He had to do this without the rest of the Feyguard.

Together, he and Brea could tackle the goblin—and then he'd have one more chance to talk with her. One more chance to understand what was really going on.

Even as the thoughts ricocheted through his head, his feet were moving. Through the cool foyer, upstairs—he skipped the elevator and took the stairs two at a time.

"House, tell the staff I need my grav-car. Immediately," he called.

"Your car is currently grounded."

"Override. It's an emergency." The staff wouldn't ask questions. And after this, he didn't care if he was grounded for life. As long as he could get to Brea in time.

In his room, he yanked open his top dresser drawer and

pulled out the dagger his dad had sent from one of his trips around the world. The ornate hilt was inlaid with emeralds, or so the accompanying note had claimed.

It didn't matter—the blade was sharp, and strong enough to pierce a goblin's skin. He slipped the blade back into the sheath, then attached it to his belt. The dagger hung at his hip, feeling surprisingly normal.

He pulled his black leather jacket from his closet and shrugged it on. Not the best armor, but better than nothing. He wished he had his Mercenary's bronze chest piece and massive sword. But this was the real world, and he had to work with what he had.

Adrenaline pumping through him, he flicked on his tablet and pulled up the satellite maps of Crestview. The Exe was a blight on the edge. Zoom in. Scan for dead trees—so many. He tilted the tablet to street-level view. No. No. There.

He stabbed the place with his finger, pinpointing it, then keyed in the directions command. Straightforward enough. He sent a copy of the directions to Jennet, along with a brief explanation. She still wasn't replying to her messager.

Tablet in one hand, he flew back down the stairs and out the front doors. The sunlight made him squint, but there was Tony, waiting with the grav-car keys beside the shiny red vehicle.

"Thanks," Roy said.

"Do you need us to summon a medic team? Where are—"

"No. I'll explain later." Roy wrenched the door open and tossed his tablet on the passenger seat.

He got to Jennet's house in record time. Engine running,

he raced to the door and pounded until it opened. Marie, the Carter's pinch-faced housekeeper, frowned at him.

"Yes?" she asked.

"I need to talk to Jennet."

"She is not at home."

Roy peered past her, but the house seemed quiet. "Where'd she go?"

"Not that it is your business, Mr. Lassiter, but she and her father have gone to visit her physical therapist."

Crap. She must have left her messager behind, or the charge had run out. It made sense, that her dad would want her checked out again, but the timing was wretched.

"Well, let her know I stopped by."

Without waiting for a reply, he dashed back to his car. Even the scant minute he'd wasted at Jennet's felt like too long.

He peeled out of the driveway. For once, all that reckless driving was going to pay off.

Brea clutched the long shard of broken glass. She had wrapped a bit of soiled rag around the end, to protect her hand. It was a poor weapon indeed, but she dared not face Codcadden unarmed.

The brick wall was cold against her back as she waited for the goblin to fall asleep. Colder still was the knowledge of her own doom. Yet she must retrieve her medallion. If the power of opening a portal between the realms fell into the goblin's hands, he would twist it to his own ends. Instead of returning to the Dark Court, he could bring his redcap tribe into the mortal world—and havoc would follow.

Only luck had left the medallion undiscovered so far.

Why had Puck entrusted her with such a thing? And why had the queen believed his assurances that Brea would return once her task was complete?

Of course, she had believed it herself, at the time. She had given her word.

But her mission remained unfulfilled, and now there was a goblin in the way. She must banish Codcadden back to the Realm of Faerie. But there could be no return for her, unless she craved the bitter banishment of the Shadowlands. No, instead she would remain in the human world, a stranded wisp of fey magic. She had no desire to carry out the Dark Queen's wishes, but she would stay, slowly fading away with every passing year.

Perhaps she could watch Roy from afar as she dwindled. And perhaps he might feel her presence, and know that she wished him no harm—only happiness, and a touch of magic to brighten his way. Her last gift to him.

The sun cast the dead tree's shadow across the ruined walls of her former shelter. After a handful of minutes, Codcadden yawned, his teeth stained with blood. He burrowed into a nest made of her shredded clothing, and closed his eyes.

Brea counted a hundred heartbeats, then a hundred more, before creeping out from the alley. Quiet as the breeze, she slid along the walls, stopping every handful of heartbeats to make sure the goblin still slumbered. The rag-wrapped glass was awkward in her hand, but she did not dare set it down.

Fear caught at her feet, rasped against her skin, yet she pressed on.

At the rough doorway, she paused, her gaze seeking the small wooden chest holding the medallion. The battered corner was visible, but lay perilously close to where the goblin slumbered.

She should wait until Codcadden departed. He was a nocturnal creature—surely he planned to go about the city that night. Her shelter would be empty, and she could claim the medallion without danger.

But what then? He was a canny creature, and would sense any trap she laid for him. Besides, if he continued to sniff out her trail, it led to Royal—and she could not bear it if he came to harm.

No, the time to act was now, before Codcadden wreaked mischief and mayhem in the human world. He slumbered heavily, sated from his meal. It would be a matter of moments to retrieve her medallion, slip it over his neck, and say the rhyme to return him to the Dark Court. Once there, its magic would be spent, at least until the queen re-infused it with power.

Her breath light as a feather in her mouth, Brea crept forward. Every few seconds she paused, eyes on Codcadden's sleeping form. When she was halfway to the chest, he grunted loudly, and she froze, fear slashing through her.

She could do this. She must.

Trembling and motionless, she waited, though her senses screamed at her to flee, to dart for the door and never return. Only the thought of Royal kept her steady—his smile, the golden glint in his brown eyes. The goblin must not be given free rein to harm him, or anyone, in the mortal world. She was the only one who could stop Codcadden.

When the goblin's breaths deepened once more, Brea continued her deliberate journey. She stepped on a blouse smeared with eye shadow, and her foot slipped. The goblin snuffled, then subsided.

After what felt like torturous hours, she finally reached the chest. Moving as if she were underwater, slow and silent, she set down her makeshift glass knife. Carefully, she removed the ruins of her second-favorite sweater from the half-buried chest, then the discarded cap of a spray bottle, then a useless wad of crumpled papers, until it was clear of debris.

She glanced at Codcadden, who slumbered on, a string of pinkish drool trailing from the corner of his mouth.

The next part was the most dangerous.

She had locked the chest with a protection spell. The moment she used her magic to open it, the goblin would wake.

She might carry the chest away, unopened, then return with the medallion and try to catch Codcadden unawares again. But he would know she had been there, would smell her passage and be doubly wary.

The time to strike was now. He lay but an arm's length away. She would open the chest, grab the medallion and fling it over his head, then chant the—blessedly short—rhyme.

Brea closed her eyes, summoning the words to the forefront of her mind.

When she opened them again, Codcadden was watching her with his evil yellow gaze.

CHAPTER TWENTY-FOUR

WITH A GASP, Brea snatched up the chest and bolted for the crumbling doorway.

Too late.

Cackling, Codcadden sprang after her. He caught her by the waist and hauled her back into the shelter. Clutching the chest under one arm, she beat and clawed at him, but he did not release her.

"I've caught a pretty fish," he said. "Clever goblin, to use such bait."

He plucked the chest from her grasp, then tossed her into the corner. She barely caught her balance in time to keep from crashing headlong into the wall, sprawling instead into a shredded pillow and the painful edge of the vid player.

"Return the chest to me," she said, rising to her knees.

"Haha! You are in no position to make demands. Now, what is inside that is so precious?"

He held the chest up and shook it, then grasped the lid and tried to pry it off. It remained stubbornly closed, and she took grim satisfaction in the fact that her spell still held against the most fearsome of redcaps.

Even when Codcadden banged it against a stone, the wood only dented. Try as he might, the goblin could not open the chest. While he strove to pry the lid open, Brea sidled toward her abandoned shard of glass. It was a poor weapon, but she would not give in without a fight.

"Tricksy girl!" he cried, rounding on her. "Open it."

"I will not."

His eyes narrowed with rage, the goblin clutched her about the neck and began to squeeze. "You will, if you want to breathe again. A dead maid's spells are easily shattered."

It was not entirely true—he would still have difficulty opening the chest. But goblins were ever full of threats. Brea kicked at him and raked her thin, human nails over his arm, to no avail. His claws dug into her skin, and bright spots danced before her eyes.

Just as the world began slipping sideways from her vision, Codcadden released her. She drew in a ragged gasp, then another, her throat painfully sore.

"Open it," he growled. "Or I shall choke you again and again, and each time you shall slip further from life."

She doubled over, coughing. When she regained her voice, she spoke, though the words were more a croak. "Very well."

He would either torture her until she opened it, or kill her and use her blood to wear away at the spell until it weakened. Since she was not yet dead, clearly she was of some use to him alive, though she shuddered to think what that use might be.

Codcadden thrust the chest at her. She held it and, after a few wavering breaths, summoned her magic. Once she held the medallion in her hands, there was a small chance she might still be able to banish him. And a small chance was better than none.

A blue flash lit her fingers, and the chest opened, spilling softer radiance into the daylight. Quickly, she drew out the medallion and threaded her fingers through its braided cord. The moonstone glimmered, the runes etched upon it shining silver.

"Oho!" The goblin leaned forward and tapped the stone with one black-clawed finger. "More than a bit of magic lies within. Tell me, little fish, what does it do?"

Brea averted her head from the fetid blast of his breath. "Put it on and see."

"You think to trick me?" He narrowed his eyes. "Wear it yourself."

She summoned a glad smile and lifted the cord over her head, as if it were a thing she had been desiring with all her heart.

"Wait," he growled, then snatched the medallion.

She yelped as the cord tangled around her fingers. The goblin tugged fiercely, abrading her skin as he pulled the medallion from her grasp. Trying not to reveal her hope, she watched as Codcadden weighed the moonstone in his hand. Its pale light dimmed, as if withdrawing from the touch of goblin flesh.

"Then again," he said, "perhaps not."

Quicker than she could follow, he tucked the medallion into a pocket sewn into his leather jerkin, then snatched her arm.

"I think it's time to consider how to best carry out the

queen's wishes," he said, leaning in close and giving her an evil leer. "Together."

"Release me." She leaned away from him, and did not have to feign her fear and disgust. But her fingers stretched, reached, touched the rag-wrapped handle of her makeshift weapon.

Scarcely breathing, she inched it toward her with her fingertips, even as Codcadden's claws dug into her other arm.

"Just a taste," he crooned, bringing his hideous face close to her cheek. He inhaled, deeply, then smacked his lips.

Before he could extend his slimy tongue, or worse yet, bite her, she grasped the glass knife and swung it around, aiming for his neck. Alas, goblin hide proved tougher than she hoped. Instead of slicing neatly across his throat, the glass point punctured him, and stuck.

"Aargh!" Codcadden yelled—but did not release his grasp.

While he still held her, she could not summon her magic and disappear, and well he knew it. He wrenched the knife from his neck, and a green trickle of blood oozed from the wound.

"I shall slice off your toes for this," he said, his eyes full of hatred. "Your pretty hands, too—and roast them over the fire."

Slowly, he drew a dagger from his belt. It was crafted of stone, but she knew it would feel sharp as steel against her skin. Brea struggled, a fish writhing desperately on the hook, well and truly caught. But she would fight until the end.

An end that was coming all too quickly. Holding her hand splayed against the cold concrete floor, Codcadden lifted his blade, ready to strike.

"Let her go!" Roy burst through the crumbling doorway, a dagger glinting in his hand.

Brea caught her breath in joyous despair at the sight of him. Somehow, he had found her! Yet, despite his metal weapon, she feared he would be no match for Codcadden.

He had the brief advantage of surprise as he lunged at the goblin. Codcadden squawked and leaped back, releasing Brea, and she scurried toward the far wall, as far from him as she could go without leaving the shelter. Her gaze went to the pocket where the medallion bulged.

"Meddlesome human," the goblin said, raising his blade. "This girl-creature is no concern of yours."

"But she is," Roy said. "And you, redcap, are even more my concern. Now, are you going to head back to the realm, or are we doing this the hard way?"

Codcadden made no reply, only leaped forward, the tip of his stone blade pointed at Roy's heart. Brea gasped, but Roy pivoted, avoiding the goblin's strike. He struck out, nicking Codcadden's shoulder.

"Thrice-blasted human!" the goblin cried. "I will gut you and eat your liver raw."

"In your dreams." Roy circled, expression grim.

One wary eye on the fight, Brea scrabbled in the debris. She must find some weapon, no matter how poor—some way to aid Roy in the fight. So far, he remained unscathed, but the goblin was a vicious and canny fighter. Fear squeezed her heart tight.

Codcadden made a giant leap into the air. He landed behind Roy, his dagger slicing through the heavy black jacket and cutting into Roy's back.

Brea's fingers closed over a heavy jar of lotion. Standing, she heaved it at Codcadden as Roy, grimacing, whirled to face his opponent.

The jar flew true, bashing Codcadden on the side of the head, and Roy went in for an attack. The goblin yelled and stumbled back, catching his foot on a tangle of white yarn that used to be a sweater.

Roy pressed the attack, and Brea scooped up several smaller containers: lip glossers, eye darkeners, lash lengtheners, vials of flowery scent. She darted closer and began pelting Codcadden, even as Roy threw himself at the goblin.

Codcadden went down, and Roy knelt on his arm, pinning the goblin's weapon, and poised his dagger at Codcadden's throat.

"No!" Brea cried. "You cannot kill him."

"Why not?" Roy's voice was tight.

"Go ahead, mortal," Codcadden hissed, his yellow eyes narrowed. "Strike your blow."

"If you spill his heart's blood here, it will only strengthen the connection to the Dark Realm." She shivered. "The queen is no stranger to blood magic, and will welcome such a solid foothold in the mortal world."

Roy swore under his breath. "Like how formally sacrificing a human in the realm would help open the gateway back to here."

He didn't sound surprised at the idea, and once again, Brea wondered what dire adventures had befallen the Feyguard in their dealings with Faerie.

"All the more reason I should have gutted you, little fish," Codcadden said, directing his words to Brea.

"Not an option." Roy tucked his blade under the goblin's chin. "Time for you to go back where you came from, redcap."

Codcadden grinned. "Alas, I cannot. The Dark Queen will not summon me back until the moon rides full upon the sky. Will you sit here for three days more, vigilantly holding a blade to my neck?"

"I have friends who'll be happy to take turns."

"And yet you are alone." Codcadden sniffed the air. "No scent or sight of another human to aid you."

"I can send him back," Brea said.

"What, you?" the goblin scoffed. "A girl most recently a trout? Indeed!"

"Shut it." Roy pressed his dagger against Codcadden's flesh, and the goblin winced.

"I will show you." Cautiously, Brea crept to the goblin's side.

The hand holding his stone dagger clenched, but Roy knelt more heavily on the goblin's arm, and Codcadden subsided. Brea found the pocket of his jerkin and yanked the medallion out, breathing shallowly to avoid the fetid goblin stench. The moonstone shimmered. Overhead, she heard the high ringing of bells.

"Ah, so that is the purpose of your pretty trinket—to return the wearer to the realm." The goblin gave her a snarling smile. "You are tricksy, but I proved the more clever."

"Okay," Roy said, glancing at Brea. "How does it work?"

In that moment of distraction, Codcadden bucked and rolled. He yanked his arm free, then shoved Roy to the ground. Before Roy could rise, the goblin punched him in the side of the head. Roy blinked woozily, trying to rise, and

Codcadden punched him again. Roy's eyes closed and he slumped to the stained concrete floor.

"No!" Brea cried, throwing herself at the goblin.

He backhanded her, the force of his blow sending her spinning into the wall. With an ugly leer, he waved his blade at Roy.

"Unlike this stupid human," he said, "I am not afraid to shed blood."

There was no time—no time to stop Codcadden, and he would never allow her to slip the medallion about his neck. No time to save both herself and Roy.

Brea pulled the medallion over her head, then staggered upright, already chanting the syllables of the rhyme. On her chest, the stone glowed and pulsed.

"By moon and chime, by sea and star."

She ran the few paces to Codcadden and wrapped her arms about him, holding fast. Since she was not attacking him, the goblin paid her little heed—all his attention fixed on the human sprawled before him. He lifted his blade.

Roy's eyes opened, then widened when he saw her clinging to the goblin.

"Across the gateway barrier."

"Brea," he whispered.

In his eyes shone the depth of his emotion, and the sight of it struck her to the core. Her voice caught on the final words, but she must say them.

The stone blade descended, the tip aimed at Roy's heart. Codcadden laughed in triumph.

"Return us from our wanderings far!"

"No!" Codcadden cried, as the magic of the realm began to swirl about them.

His knife pierced Roy's chest—but it was no longer a deadly blade. It was a wisp of nightmare, of dream. Roy winced, but no blood spurted forth.

The goblin thrashed in fury, his black claws gouging long furrows in her arms, but she kept her grip locked tight. Through the fading air, her gaze met Roy's.

"I love you," he said.

"And I you." The truth of it resonated through her with a brightness that made her want to weep.

"Don't go!" His voice was raw with anguish as he reached, his hands passing through her like smoke.

"I will await you on the far shore, my love." It was the only promise she could make.

The goblin snarled. "You will pay for this, little fish, as soon as we return to the court."

"I know it." But her heart had already paid the price, a thousand times over.

Her last sight of the mortal world was Roy on his knees, arms outstretched toward an impossible future. His cheeks were glazed with tears, then with silver as the twilight moon broke free of the clouds and shone, impervious to human heartbreak, over the lost souls of the Exe.

CHAPTER TWENTY-FIVE

"Brea!" Roy's voice cracked as she, and the goblin, disappeared in a flash of silvery light.

Heart racing, he jumped to his feet. If he hurried home, logged in to Feyland, could he make it all the way to the Dark Court in time to save her?

He didn't know, but he had to try. Pushing back the knowledge that facing the Dark Queen would be suicide, he slipped his dagger into the sheath on his belt. As he did, he felt a faint warmth in his pocket. The crystal tear!

He pulled it out, fingers unsteady. Had Brea somehow returned?

The inside of the crystal glowed, and an image of Brea formed there, but it was static, like a portrait. White blossoms glimmered in her hair, and she wore her usual serious expression.

He stared at it for several heartbeats, but the picture never changed. He tucked it back into his jeans.

It was a memento, a memory—but he couldn't be content

with that. Not when there was still a chance he could rescue her from whatever dire fate awaited her in the realm. His messenger was in the car. The rest of the Feyguard would come help him. He hoped.

He stepped over the piles of shredded clothing, then paused at the sound of voices. Strangely, as if thinking about them had conjured them up, it sounded like his friends.

Friends, or foe, somebody was approaching. Drawing his dagger again, he hurried to the gaping doorway of the ruined house and peered outside.

Tam, Jennet, Marny, and Tam's little brother—affectionately called the Bug—stood partway down the nearby alley.

"We're here," the Bug said.

"Are you sure?" Tam glanced around, his stance wary.

Jennet looked nervous. "We're pretty deep in the Exe. I wish you hadn't made George wait so far away."

"A grav-car like that, cruising around the Exe, would only draw trouble," Tam said. "Bug, I don't see anything, and it's getting dark."

"Trust the little guy," Marny said. "After all, we've followed him this far."

"Over here," Roy called softly, stepping out the door.

Tam's head snapped up. He motioned the others behind him, and they closed the distance to where Roy stood.

"How do we know you're actually Roy?" Tam asked.

Marny nodded. "Good point. Tell us something that only Roy would know."

It was smart of them. Roy firmed his lips and thought.

"Okay," he said. "The first time Tam and I dueled in a game, we made the same characters, but his was female."

Jennet smiled, and Tam gave him a grudging nod.

"So, where's the goblin?" Marny asked, pointedly looking into the ruined house. "Bug insisted you and Brea were in mortal danger."

"The goblin's been sent back to the realm," Roy said.

"They were in trouble," the Bug piped up. "But now everything's fine."

"Great." Tam shot his little brother a look. "You couldn't have mentioned that earlier?"

The kid blinked from beneath his tousled brown hair. "But then I wouldn't have gotten to ride in the grav-car."

"The important thing is that you're safe," Jennet said, interrupting Tam's annoyed inhale. "What happened? Where's Brea?"

"She's gone, too." Urgency overrode the pain inside him. "She saved me, and sacrificed herself to take the redcap back. We have to go in and save her. Now."

Tam and Jennet exchanged a quick look, and then Jennet set her hand on Roy's arm.

"She's from the realm. I don't think the Feyguard have much power to interfere in the affairs of the fey folk."

"But she's going to be banished!"

His words echoed in the dim alley, and Tam glanced around.

"We need to go," he said. "The Exe at dusk is not the place to stand around having a chat."

"I have my car," Roy said. "We can all squeeze in and go to my house."

Marny gave him a doubtful look, but he ignored her.

"Your car is here?" Jennet asked him.

"Down the street and around the corner," Roy said. "Though it may be gone by now."

"Not yet," the Bug said. "But somebody saw it and is coming back."

It was freaky, the way the kid knew things, but at the moment, Roy was glad of his ability. He glanced at the quickly darkening sky, and shivered.

"Then let's hurry."

He led the way, stumbling over the rubble littering the ground. The goblin had punched him pretty hard in the head, but at least his vision was clear, even if his balance was a little off. His skull hurt, but it was nothing compared to his heart.

A small hand slipped into his. Startled, Roy glanced down to see Tam's little brother beside him. The kid looked up, a depth of sympathy in his eyes that seemed misplaced in someone so young.

"It will all be okay," he said in a solemn voice.

"I hope so."

Something howled into the night, and Roy sprinted the last few paces, unlocking the car as soon as his keys were in range. He slid into the driver's seat and fired up the ignition.

"Quick," Tam urged, as they all piled in.

He, Jennet, and the Bug squeezed in back, Marny in the passenger seat. The doors slamming sounded too loud, and Roy hastily activated the locks. As he turned the car, the headlights swept across a clump of young men holding clubs. Their eyes flashed in the reflected light.

"Gang," Tam said. "Step on it."

Roy didn't need any encouragement. He hit the accelerator, the engine roaring. The gang members yelled, and one threw a rock that struck the car with a thud, but Roy didn't stop.

"Head to Zeg's," Marny said. "It's closer."

"He got his FullD systems in?" Tam asked.

"Installed yesterday," Marny said.

Roy sped out of the Exe, grateful for the grav technology that enabled him to skim over the yawning potholes and pitted concrete.

"Do you think they'll work for us?" Jennet asked, doubt clear in her voice.

"Hey." Marny turned around to look at Jennet. "My uncle's a Feyguard too, you know. They'll work."

Roy didn't waste his breath on speculation. All his attention was focused on getting into the realm, and getting Brea out.

Then what? a voice inside him asked. *What's a faerie girl going to do, trapped in the human world?*

He didn't have an answer—just the aching emptiness inside when he thought of Brea.

After what felt like an hour, but was closer to ten minutes, Roy pulled up outside the simcafé. The sign was turned to *Closed*, but Marny slid her key into the lock, and the door opened. The bells overhead gave a merry jingle as they trooped inside, and Roy finally let out his breath.

"Well, hello," Zeg said, coming in from the kitchen. He didn't look too surprised to see them. "Tea? Cookies?"

"Yes, please!" said the Bug. He hopped into a nearby booth and sat, wiggling with anticipation.

"We need to use the FullD systems," Roy said.

Zeg pursed his lips, but nodded. "They're in the way back."

"I'll stay here with the Bug," Marny said. "Good luck."

"Roy," Jennet said as Zeg led them to the sim systems, "this might not be the best idea."

"I don't care. We have to try."

Zeg handed him a brand-new helmet and pair of gloves. "You have loyal friends," he said. "But don't get them killed."

That made Roy pause. He made himself slow down and really think about what he was doing. Was it worth putting his friends in mortal danger to save a creature of the Dark Realm? Even one he loved?

"Maybe you guys are right," he said. "I'll go in alone."

"Look," Tam said. "We're here, we've got gear. We'll all go in and see."

"Not too far," Zeg warned.

"We'll be careful," Jennet said, settling into the sim chair. "See you in there."

The golden light tipped through Roy, and he welcomed the queasy sensation. An instant later, his Mercenary stood in the faerie ring, with Tam's Knight and Jennet's Spellcaster beside him. Damn, Zeg was right. He was lucky to have such prime friends.

"Wait." Tam held up one hand. "Something's coming."

The underbrush on the Dark Realm's side of the clearing rustled. Roy drew his sword. His pulse thudded in his ears. What if it was the goblin, with the rest of his tribe?

Jennet lifted her staff, the crystal shedding blue light into the shadows. Into that glow, a figure tumbled, tangle-haired and bright-eyed.

"Puck." Roy took a step forward. "Where is Brea? And don't pretend you don't know her this time."

The sprite tilted his head and rose into the air until he could look Roy in the eye.

"Alas," Puck said. "She is beyond your reach, mortal boy."

"No!" Roy's heart wrenched, the pain he'd been walling off flowing fresh as blood. "We're here to save her." *Too late.*

"She is not a creature of your world," the sprite said. "There is naught you can do to avert her fate."

"But—"

"I must go—and if you three value your lives, you will depart as well. The queen is full of ire and wrath, and her senses will fasten upon your presence here, ere long." Puck glanced over his shoulder, then leaped into the air.

A snowy white owl swooped through the trees, catching him upon its back. The sprite raised his long-fingered hand as the owl bore him away.

"Go now!" he cried. "Danger stirs."

The pale bird disappeared into the shadows beneath the trees. A cold wind blew through the clearing, whipping the silver-leafed branches. Black clouds piled overhead, and the forest darkened.

"Well?" Tam asked, turning to Roy. "Stay, or go?"

Roy peered down the pathway leading to the Dark Court, his emotions clashing.

"I can't ask you to do this," he finally said.

"You don't have to." Jennet planted her staff firmly on the velvet green mosses. "We're with you. Now let's go find Brea."

CHAPTER TWENTY-SIX

B<small>REA BENT</small> and wrapped her arms about herself, huddling before the force of the Dark Queen's icy wrath. Frost sparkled on the velvet moss beneath her feet, and the air sliced her lungs with bitter cold. The back of her neck burned, where the queen had snatched the medallion from her with such force the cord had broken.

"How dare you return to the realm unsuccessful!" The Dark Queen pointed one long, pale finger at Brea, and then at the goblin crouched beside her. "And you, Codcadden—bested by a mere mortal."

Clenching her hand into a fist, the queen whirled about in her anger, her dark skirts brushing the foliage surrounding the Dark Court's clearing. Night-blooming flowers shriveled in her wake.

"My queen," Codcadden said, his voice oily with supplication. "This stupid fish-girl forced me to return—and on the cusp of victory. Had I slain the mortal boy and supped of his blood, my powers would have been magnified threefold. Think of what I could have done."

"On *my* behalf," the queen said, narrowing her eyes at the goblin. "Do not overstep, redcap."

Brea shivered, and not just from the cold. The thought of Codcadden wreaking havoc in the mortal world was too gruesome to contemplate. Not only had she saved Roy, she'd spared his city from a killing spree.

"Forgive me, your majesty." The goblin prostrated himself on the ground.

The queen regarded him for a long moment, then waved her hand. "Get thee gone from my court, redcap, and do not return for a handful of moons, lest you crave my ire."

Codcadden crawled backward, not looking up until he'd removed himself from the vicinity of the tangled throne. A goblin's companionship was not much to speak of, but now Brea was left to face the queen alone. She pressed her fingernails into her palms, and lifted her head.

"You." The queen drew a long black thorn from her sleeve and ran her pale fingers back and forth along it. "Were I not bound by my word, your cold blood would spill in service to my court. But alas, banishment it will be, and not death. Still, the Shadowlands are not kind to those who dwell therein. Say your farewell to the realm, silver trout."

She lifted her hand, violet sparks glowing in her palm.

Blinking past unexpected tears, Brea cast a final look about the Dark Court. Moonlight filtered through the tree branches, its light vying with the flickering purple flames of the bonfire and the pixie-trapped lanterns. The oaks sighed in the wind, and beneath the boughs the denizens of the court stood, solemn.

The gossamer-winged maidens, the ragged banshee, the feral sprites—all of them watched her, uneasy and unspeaking. Brea had no allies, no friends among the court to remember her when she was gone. Her light would wink out from the realm, unremarked upon, unmourned.

Then a figure stepped forth, his eyes merry despite the occasion. Puck, garbed in leaves and tatters. Her heart lightened the smallest bit at the sight of him.

"Farewell, Brea Cairgead. May the moonlight guide your way." He swept her a bow.

Not trusting her voice, Brea returned the gesture, then took one last breath of the sweet night air.

"For breaking your word, I cast thee out," the Dark Queen said, raising her glowing hands. "For returning to the realm, your task unfulfilled." She flung her hands wide, and the frost of her magic engulfed Brea. "By star and by branch, by seed and by wither, I send thee into the Shadowlands —forever!"

The Dark Court wavered, as though it were a reflection stirred by the wind. Brea closed her eyes and braced herself for the desolation of her exile.

When she opened them again, she still stood in the court. Confusion thrashed in her chest, and she glanced at Puck. He winked at her.

"Begone!" the queen cried, once again flinging her magic forth.

This time, the court remained solid. A tiny flicker of hope lit within Brea.

"I banish thee!" The queen's voice was strident now. Dark clouds gathered, eclipsing the moon.

Yet Brea remained.

Puck leaped up, ascending the air until he reached Brea's shoulder. He gave the queen a flourishing bow.

"Allow me to explain, milady," he said.

"Do so," the queen hissed. Blue and violet light crackled about her midnight figure.

"I was present when you commanded the fish-girl to go into the mortal world and use her magic to make the humans susceptible to the realm."

"And she failed!" The queen lifted her hands again, pale fingers crooked.

"Ah, but she did not." Puck set one finger to his cheek and grinned. "Else you would have been able to send her forth from the realm. Since you cannot, then she did not break her word."

"How can this be? Bard Thomas, answer me true," the queen demanded.

The bard stepped forward and regarded Brea from his wise and weary eyes.

"I would venture to say yon fish has captured a human heart—one already susceptible to fey magic. And one who will somehow strengthen the Realm of Faerie's presence in the mortal world. The balance between the realms has shifted. Nearly imperceptibly, but if it had not, the girl would now be wandering the Shadowlands."

"It is not what I desired." The queen's eyes narrowed. "She was to bring me mortals via the human game of Feyland, so that the realm might live on."

Puck somersaulted through the air, this time alighting near the bard. The rest of the court remained still and watchful, even the breeze dying to a faint motion of shadowed air.

"Perhaps you craved too much," the sprite said—the only member of the queen's court who would dare to say such a thing. "Somehow, the little fish has succeeded in opening the realm to human dreams and wishes."

"Dreams and wishes!" The queen clenched her hands. "Blood is what I require. I do not need another poet or playwright wandering the world, fey-touched. I need a sacrifice."

"And yet, you did not say so when you set the geas upon your subject." Bard Thomas's tone was mild, but there was a spark in his eye. Was he pleased to see his ruler thwarted? "Without a touch of mortal essence, the realm will wither, aye. But whether that mortality is blood red or the silver mist of longing and vision, the magic cares not. It will replenish either way. And so, the fish-girl has succeeded."

Brea stood motionless, barely breathing. If Thomas spoke true, then the folly of losing her heart to Roy was no folly at all, but the very thing that had saved her. His belief in the realm and his love for her would somehow allow a trickle of essential energy to flow into the Realm of Faerie. Enough to keep them from fading away.

She smiled, a small, secret curve of her lips. Aye, the queen wanted power and domination, but she would have to be content with much less.

The queen turned to Brea, fury still covering her unearthly face. She cast a handful of magic over Brea, the power sifting down and lodging in her bones.

"Should you ever attempt to return to the mortal world,"

the queen said, "you will lose your girl form and become your true self. Now, depart from my court—but every seven years you must return and I shall speak the banishing spell. If your human lover fails to maintain his connection with the Realm of Faerie, you will find yourself wandering the Shadowlands."

"As you command." Brea dipped her head and performed the most elegant curtsy she could manage.

She had escaped her fate. Perhaps it was only a reprieve, but the warm heart of her believed in Royal, believed that the bond between them would remain unbroken. Somehow.

"Go!" The queen slashed her hand through the air.

Brea turned and fled—past the shambling trolls and grinning spriggans, past the wraith-pale water maids and night-black kelpies. She plunged into the shadows between the tall oak trees, her back prickling as though the queen might send a final, fatal bolt of magic at her as she ran.

But no strike came, and soon the court fell away behind her. Still, she did not rest, fear and hope in equal measure carrying her across moon-dappled meadows and beside the silver thread of a streamlet.

Ahead, in the distance, she glimpsed a blue light. Though she was loath to leave the comfort of the stream, the glow called to her. Carefully, she turned her steps, heart pounding. Perhaps it was only a will-o-wisp, beckoning her into the mists. Yet she could not deny the tug upon her.

The light strengthened, outlining the path between the trees. Faintly, she heard the sound of mortal voices. Could it be?

Cautiously, she slipped under the tent-like branches of a nearby hemlock. The blue glow grew closer, bobbing up and down, until she could make out the three figures striding along the path. She leaned forward, scarcely breathing, and her chest clenched in joy at the sight of Royal and his friends.

"Hold up." Roy paused on the path, his bared sword shining. "I heard something."

Jennet lifted her staff. "Where?"

Taking her courage in her hands, Brea stepped out from the sheltering screen of the evergreen tree.

"Here," she said.

"Brea!" Roy started forward, but Tam caught his arm.

"Maybe, maybe not. Ask her a question."

Jennet nodded, and Roy paused, his eyes fixed on Brea's. Even in the dim light, she could see the emotion shining there.

"Where did I take you, in the mortal world?" he asked.

"The waterfall," she answered.

"It's her," Roy said.

He pulled from Tam's hold and ran the few paces to where Brea stood.

"I never thought I'd see you again," he said, folding her in his arms.

She returned his embrace, the unaccustomed moisture of tears wetting her face. "Nor I, you."

Brea leaned into his warmth and strength, letting all her fears and sorrows subside for that one moment. There was only breath and body and the echo of two heartbeats.

"This is too easy," Tam said. "I thought Puck said Brea was gone."

"I nearly was." She lifted her face to Roy's. "But the queen could not banish me."

"Then you can come back with us," he said, his smile brilliant as the sunrise.

She stiffened. "Alas love, but I cannot."

"What?" He stared down at her, hurt darkening his eyes. "I mean, I know there will be some issues, since I'm human and you're fey, but—"

Brea stopped his words by laying one finger across his mouth. "The queen set her magic upon me. If I return to the human world, I will revert to my true form."

"I don't care," he said. "I'll love you, even if you're hideous."

"It is more than that." She sighed, and for a moment heard the streamlet in the distance sigh back at her. "I cannot breathe air when I am in that shape. Nor can I converse or use my hands, for I have neither tongue nor fingers."

"Oh. That makes things a little difficult." He was trying to jest, but his voice cracked on the words.

"But you can be a girl in the realm and in Feyland, right?" Jennet asked.

"Aye." Hope was a brief spark within her, one that could catch fire, or burn down just as quickly to ash.

"Then we could meet." Roy took her hands and squeezed them hopefully. "I'll come and visit you every day."

"The queen would take notice of that, I fear. Mayhap once a month would not draw her attention."

"That's not enough. I don't want to lose you at all." Roy's voice was taut with longing.

Brea pulled her hand from his, then placed it over his heart. "I dwell here, Royal. I am always with you."

A single tear spilled from his eye. She caught it on her finger and brought it to her lips, tasting his salt.

"Now I'm in you, too." He gave her a crooked smile.

"Always. And every full moon, when the queen's power wanes beneath the light, we shall meet here, in the realm."

Roy shook his head and pulled her tightly against him, but he ceased arguing. Her soul weeping, Brea breathed deeply of his mortal scent. Salt and spice. Love.

"Ahaha!" A deep laugh boomed through the forest. "A pretty sight. And now you mortals may spend your blood in service to the queen's wishes."

Brea gasped. Roy thrust her behind him and drew his sword as the Black Knight advanced out of the shadows.

CHAPTER TWENTY-SEVEN

Roy GRIPPED his sword and took a deep breath. Ah, crap. He'd managed to put himself and nearly everyone he cared about directly into the Black Knight's path.

"Stay back," he said to Brea. "No heroics this time, okay?"

She nodded, wide-eyed, as Tam and Jennet moved up to flank him.

"Sorry, guys," he said.

"Hey, we defeated him once before." Tam settled his shield on his arm and hefted his sword.

"Although it looks like he brought reinforcements." Jennet sounded a little worried.

She tipped her staff forward, and the pale blue light illuminated a score of creatures advancing along the path. Some were hunched over and covered with lichens and moss, others capered on long, twiggy limbs. A redcap goblin looked at Roy and gave an evil grin.

"My kin have a debt to settle with you, mortal!" he called, brandishing his serrated spear.

Behind the ragtag army, the Black Knight sat astride a coal-black steed. His eyes were lit with green fire.

"Take them!" he cried in his sepulchral voice.

Screaming and wailing, the creatures swarmed forward.

Tam and Roy moved up to meet them, swinging their swords in rhythm. A sheet of flame poured over their enemies, and the long-limbed creatures shrieked with dismay, though the goblins and hobs seemed unaffected.

The redcap marched toward Roy, trampling a fallen ally. He stabbed forward with his spear. Roy knocked it aside, but it had been a ploy. The goblin dropped his weapon and leaped at Roy, a knife in his hand, pointed directly at the vulnerable spot where Roy's chest plate met his shoulder armor. Dammit. No time to get his sword back around to deflect the blow.

With a shout, he twisted aside. The goblin's knife grated against Roy's bronze armor, but missed the target by a mere inch. The redcap howled in fury and sprang toward Roy's face, claws curved in attack. The edge of Tam's shield clipped the goblin on the head and he went down.

"Enough!" the Black Knight cried. "The queen wants them alive."

His minions drew back a few paces, their weapons at the ready, their eyes bright and malicious.

"Yeah, so that she can kill us herself," Tam said. "No thanks."

"Run for it?" Jennet whispered. "We're not that far from the clearing."

"We can keep fighting," Roy said.

A long, wavering howl undulated through the night sky. The knight lifted his mangled face to the stars and called back.

The excited yipping of hounds answered him, and the distant thunder of hoof beats.

"Or not," Roy added.

"You cannot defeat the entire hunt," Brea said in a quiet voice. "I shall make a distraction while you flee."

"No heroics," Roy said. "Dammit, Brea."

"I will be careful. And I am fey. Make ready."

He leaned back and kissed her on the lips. The watching creatures snickered.

"One last embrace before you meet your doom?" the knight called. "How quaint."

The warmth of Roy's kiss still lingering on her mouth, Brea lifted her hands and began to sing. She called the droplets from the trees, the water from the streamlet. She drew strength from the warmth of friendship surrounding her, from Roy's kiss, from the marvelous and tragic circumstances of their love. Her voice rose, carried through the trees.

"Stop her!" the Black Knight cried.

Roy and Tam and Jennet leaped to defend her, battling back the creatures that sought her life. Fireballs and swords flashed, and still Brea sang, coaxing the watery depths to rise and come to her. The ground beneath her feet grew damp, then wetter. The battle about her filled with splashes and fey curses as overhead the eerie light of the Wild Hunt illuminated the sky.

She finished her song. "Make ready!" she called, then brought her hands together in a mighty clap.

Water rushed from her right and left, two waves crashing through the trees, the trunks doing nothing to hold them back. The Black Knight howled in denial as his soldiers were swept by the current.

"Go!" she cried to the humans.

"I love you," Roy called, his words nearly lost beneath the sound of rushing water.

Then he and his friends turned and pelted down the path, away from her and toward the safety of the mortal world.

Brea clapped again, this time loosing her anguish and despair. The waves leaped, higher than the Black Knight's head. Yet they did not deter him as he drew his sword and galloped toward her, hollow eyes alight with wrath.

Once more she crashed the waves together, and then let go her mortal shape. The knight's blade whipped down, but she was flashing silver, she was fin and ripple. She was gone, speeding to safety even as the waves receded, letting the water bear her home.

Roy sat in the sim chair at Zeg's, senses reeling. The ache running through him knotted his stomach, and every muscle in his body. He felt like he'd been poisoned. And yet, would he really give up the pain, the memory of Brea's face, of her kiss?

He'd lost her, then found her, then lost her once again. *It's not fair!*

He wanted to plunge back into the game, but that would be idiotic. Even if he made it back, Brea wouldn't be there. Not until the full moon.

Before logging out, he'd lagged behind the others, despite Jennet's desperate insistences. He'd seen that moment of transformation as a glimmering silver trout plunged into the waves, nimbly avoiding the Black Knight's strike. She'd escaped, and he had to believe he'd see her again.

Tam and Jennet had their gear off. Without saying anything, they headed back into the main room of the café. Tam patted Roy's shoulder in passing, and Jennet squeezed his arm as they left him to his privacy. He didn't care if they'd seen the tears wetting his eyes.

He'd fallen in love with a fey girl who was really a fish. And it didn't matter one bit. His heart was still breaking, but somehow he'd get up out of the sim chair and make it through the night. And the next one, and the one after that, until finally the moon rose full and round.

He stood and pulled the teardrop out of his pocket. The image of Brea was still captured within. At least he had some tiny part of her left in the mortal world. Heaving a deep sigh, he tucked the teardrop away. Time to go deal with the real world.

A mug of tea and a cookie waited for him along with his friends. The Bug scooted over in the booth to make room, and Roy sat, feeling more tired than he had in weeks.

"Thanks," he said, to all of them in general.

Marny patted his shoulder. "Tam and Jennet filled me in," she said. "I'm sorry."

"Well, you were right. And I was an idiot. Again." He took a bite of cookie. It was flavorless, but he kept chewing.

Jennet reached across the table and squeezed his hand, her eyes full of wordless understanding. "We all screw up."

"And we managed to do our job as Feyguard," Tam said. "Though it didn't quite work out for the best."

Roy wrapped his hands around his mug of tea, trying to absorb some of the warmth. It felt like nothing would ever fill the cold loneliness inside him.

"Don't worry," the Bug said in his high, piping voice. "She will always be there, waiting for you."

"I hope so."

In memory, Brea smiled at him beside the waterfall, water like pearls in her dark hair, her eyes filled with silver mystery. His muse. His true love.

EPILOGUE

Swirling golden light surrounded Roy. When it cleared, he found himself standing in a twilight clearing, a ring of pale mushrooms surrounding him. Overhead, the full moon rode high above wispy clouds.

Sweet music drifted through the shadowed trees, and he glimpsed the figure of a bard picking out a melody on his battered guitar. Small, glowing creatures darted through the air—pixies, their high laughter chiming in counterpoint.

At the edge of the clearing a tattered sprite with merry eyes sat cross-legged on a white-speckled toadstool. He stood and swept Roy a bow.

"Welcome again to the realm, Royal One," Puck said. "There is one here awaiting you."

He gestured, and Roy turned to see a faerie maiden, her pale skin glimmering, apple blossoms tangled in her hair. His heart ached with perfect joy.

"Brea."

She smiled and held out her hands. "My love. Come with me. Until moonset, the realm awaits."

Roy stepped out of the faerie ring and folded her into his embrace. A sweet wind moved over the silver-leaved trees.

Fingers entwined, without looking back, Brea and Royal strode together into the bright dark of the Realm of Faerie.

SONG OF THE WANDERING AENGUS

W.B YEATS

I went out to the hazel wood,
Because a fire was in my head,
And cut and peeled a hazel wand,
And hooked a berry to a thread,
And when white moths were on the wing,
And moth-like stars were flickering out,
I dropped the berry in a stream
And caught a little silver trout.

When I had laid it on the floor
I went to blow the fire a-flame,
But something rustled on the floor,
And someone called me by my name:
It had become a glimmering girl
With apple blossom in her hair
Who called me by my name and ran
And faded through the brightening air.

Though I am old with wandering
Through hollow lands and hilly lands,
I will find out where she has gone,
And kiss her lips and take her hands;
And walk among long dappled grass,
And pluck till time and times are done,
The silver apples of the moon.
The golden apples of the sun.

ACKNOWLEDGEMENTS

Thank you to the many people who made this book better: the invaluable feedback of my CP Chassily and fabulous first readers Marissa and Brynn, and my fine editor, Laurie Temple. Thanks also to Arran at Editing720 for quick, professional, and stellar proofreading.

For another fabulous cover, huge thanks to Ravven. And for the inspiration to move forward, ongoing gratitude to all the indie authors and publishers who share their journey so generously.

I also greatly appreciate the readers who have taken the time to contact me, leave reviews, and give me reasons to keep writing. This series wouldn't be here without you! Thank you.

ROYAL draws on a number of traditional resources, including my go-to books for Faerie lore: *An encyclopedia of fairies: Hobgoblins, brownies, bogies, and other supernatural crea-*

tures by Katharine M. Briggs, and *Faeries* by Froud, Larkin, and Lee.

Readers will also find references to a variety of fairy tales and story archetypes, as well as the poem Song of the Wandering Aengus by W.B. Yeats.

OTHER WORKS

THE FEYLAND SERIES

What if a high-tech game was a gateway to the treacherous Realm of Faerie?

THE FIRST ADVENTURE - Book 0 (prequel)

THE DARK REALM – Book 1

THE BRIGHT COURT – Book 2

THE TWILIGHT KINGDOM – Book 3

FAERIE SWAP - Book 3.5

TRINKET (short story)

SPARK - Book 4

BREAS'S TALE - Book 4.5

ROYAL - Book 5

MARNY - Book 6

CHRONICLE WORLDS: FEYLAND

FEYLAND TALES: Volume 1

VICTORIA ETERNAL

Steampunk meets Space Opera in a British Galactic Empire that never was...

PASSAGE OUT

STAR COMPASS

STARS & STEAM

COMETS & CORSETS

THE DARKWOOD CHRONICLES

Deep in the Darkwood, a magical doorway leads to the enchanted and dangerous land of the Dark Elves~

ELFHAME

HAWTHORNE

RAINE

HEART of the FOREST (novella)

WHITE AS FROST

BLACK AS NIGHT

RED AS FLAME

SHORT STORY COLLECTIONS

TALES OF FEYLAND & FAERIE

TALES OF MUSIC & MAGIC

THE FAERIE GIRL & OTHER TALES

THE PERFECT PERFUME & OTHER TALES

COFFEE & CHANGE

MERMAID SONG

ABOUT THE AUTHOR

Growing up, Anthea Sharp spent most of her summers raiding the library shelves and reading, especially fantasy. She now makes her home in the sunny Southern California, where she writes, plays the fiddle, and tries not to game *too* much. Visit her website at antheasharp.com, friend her on Facebook, and be the first to know about new releases and reader perks by subscribing to Anthea's new release newsletter, Sharp Tales, at www.subscribepage.com/AntheaSharp